D0786420

The Magical Animal Adoption Agency

2 THE ENCHANTED EGG

ALSO BY KALLIE GEORGE

The Magical Animal Adoption Agency, Book 1: Clover's Luck

BY **Kallie George**

ILLUSTRATED BY
Alexandra Boiger

DISNEY • HYPERION
LOS ANGELES NEW YORK

First Edition, November 2015
10 9 8 7 6 5 4 3 2 1
FAC-020093-15227
Printed in the United States of America

Library of Congress Cataloging-in-Publication Data
George, Kallie.
The enchanted egg / by Kallie George ; illustrated by Alexandra Boiger.
—First edition.
pages cm.—(The Magical Animal Adoption Agency ; 2)
Summary: "Clover receives a mysterious egg at the Magical Animal
Adoption Agency"—Provided by publisher.
ISBN 978-1-4231-8383-9—ISBN 1-4231-8383-5
[1. Eggs—Fiction. 2. Imaginary creatures—Fiction. 3. Pet adoption—
Fiction. 4. Magic—Fiction. 5. Animals—Infancy—Fiction.]
I. Boiger, Alexandra, illustrator. II. Title.
PZ7.G293326Enc 2015
[Fic]—dc23 2014037749

Reinforced binding

Visit www.DisneyBooks.com

THIS LABEL APPLIES TO TEXT STOCK

Dedicated to my dad, who taught me how to make cinnamon toast

—K.G.

To Charmian, with love

—A.B.

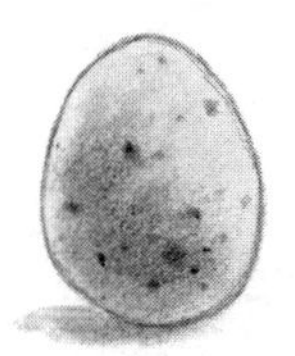

Contents

1

The Egg

An egg is full of possibilities. Especially an enchanted one. The tiniest egg can hold the most fearsome dragon. The biggest egg, the shiest sea serpent.

What was inside the giant spotted egg at the Agency was a total mystery. Clover knew it couldn't be a dragon. Mr. Jams, who ran the Agency, had said so. And he knew lots about dragon eggs. It couldn't be a sea serpent either. Sea serpents make sloshing noises inside their shells. The egg was too large to be a fire salamander's and too golden for a griffin's. And phoenixes don't even hatch from eggs. They rise from their ashes.

Really, it didn't matter what the egg contained. Clover loved it already.

It was another hot summer morning as Clover skipped up Dragon's Tail Lane, toward the Agency. From the outside, the low wooden building didn't look special at all, with its crooked chimney, vine-covered walls, and thatched roof. But inside was another thing altogether. From its sign reading NO ANIMAL IS TOO UNUSUAL TO ADOPT, to the big gilt Wish Book, to the animals themselves—fire salamanders, fairy horses,

unicorns, and other magical creatures—the Agency was a remarkable place.

You never knew what might happen in a day. Clover had only been volunteering there since the beginning of summer vacation, three weeks ago, and already she had adopted out a unicorn and a dragon and rescued a little kitten from a nasty witch. New homes found, friends made, and hearts healed—that was the Agency. And now there was the egg, which wasn't up for adoption yet, of course, but the animal that hatched from it would be, as soon as it was old enough.

Clover hurried through the gate. "Morning," she said to the garden gnome who stood beside it. Although he looked like a lawn ornament, he was actually alive. He guarded the Agency at night and slept through the day. In fact, Clover realized he was asleep now, so she was careful not to bang the gate shut behind her.

Mr. Jams had the lights on in the front room, but the Agency didn't open for another hour. Clover headed around the building. The egg was kept in one of the pens in the back, in the stables. Usually these pens were reserved for the bigger animals, like dragons or griffins, but the Agency didn't have any big magical animals at the moment, so the pen was nice and quiet, perfect for an egg.

The back door of the Agency was hidden by dark green vines. The vines gave the door a secret feel, which Clover liked.

She pushed them aside to find the keyhole and stuck in the tiny key made from a tooth. She used to wear the key on a string around her wrist, but now it hung around her neck, tucked under her clothes, safely out of sight. Mr. Jams had given it to her when he'd left her in charge and gone to rescue the egg. When she'd offered to give the key back, he told her it was hers. "You've earned it," he'd said.

The door creaked open and Clover squeezed through between two pens, into the sweet smell of hay, the sound of the unicorns' soft whinnies, and the sight of thousands of fluffy feathers.

The egg's pen was in the center of the stables beside the hay room, and was filled, knee-high, with different types of feathers. Mr. Jams had determined that this was the best way of keeping the egg warm and safe. It looked like hundreds of pillows had burst and no one had cleaned up the mess. From the center of the feathers poked a yellow-and-white-spotted lump. The egg was really big—bigger than a watermelon—but you would never know because of all the feathers that hid it.

On the edge of the pen stood the little green kitten Clover had saved from the witch, staring longingly at the feathers with his emerald eyes.

"Oh, Dipity, you silly thing." Clover rubbed behind his ears. She was grateful that Mr. Jams let her keep him at the Agency as her pet. She couldn't bear it if he was adopted by someone else.

She set her bag on the ground and pulled out her baby blanket. It was a soft fleece and she wanted to add it to the nest.

Yesterday she had brought a book and read to the egg for a whole hour because she had heard that reading to babies before they were born helped them develop. Now that Mr. Jams had returned from his mission to rescue the abandoned egg, she had more time to do fun things like that with the animals—things like taking the fire salamanders out for sunbathing and riding the unicorns for exercise. She even got to meet the delivery-man who brought them supplies. And he wasn't a man at all—he was a centaur!

"Stay, Dipity," she ordered her kitten as she opened the pen door. Dipity liked pouncing on the feathers, but he wasn't allowed to, in case he harmed the egg.

Clover waded through the soft fluff, carrying her

baby blanket. The feathers tickled her legs. When she reached the egg, she tucked the blanket around its base, in the nest Mr. Jams had made from twigs and twine, so the egg would sit upright.

She pressed her palm against the warm shell. Although it looked hard and smooth, like most eggshells, it wasn't. This shell felt soft as velvet, like a unicorn's muzzle. As Clover stroked the strange, velvety egg for the thousandth time, she promised: "I will take care of you."

The egg, Mr. Jams had told her, was found by a troll family under their drawbridge, hidden in some brambles. It had obviously been abandoned, but a protective enchantment had been placed on it so that no harm would come to the egg. But whatever hatched out of it would be left to fend for itself. That's why the trolls had contacted the Agency. It had taken Mr. Jams a day and a half to travel to the trolls' home. Once he'd released the egg from the enchantment and rescued it from the brambles, they'd insisted he stay for a troll family feast before he brought it back to the Agency. Although Mr. Jams had examined the area around the drawbridge thoroughly for clues as to what type of animal had laid the egg, he found nothing. Clover felt sorry that the egg didn't have its mother to look after it, but she was glad that at least it was now somewhere it would be cared for.

She continued stroking the egg until Dipity mewed hungrily. It was time to get on with the day. She was just opening the pen door when—yes, she was sure of it—out of the corner of her eye, she saw the egg move.

She turned back toward it.

The egg was perfectly still.

She tiptoed over and knelt to place her ear against the shell. All she could hear was the beating of her own heart. She waited a minute, then let out a deep breath and stood up.

Dipity remained at the gate of the pen, his green eyes locked on the egg.

"Did you see that too?" asked Clover.

The little green kitten didn't look up at her, but his tail twitched into the shape of a question mark.

2

Mr. Jams's Journey

Clover hurried down the hall and into the front room of the Agency, with Dipity following. The smell of buttery toast let Clover know that Mr. Jams was there. He would know what to do.

"Mr. Jams, the egg moved! I saw it!" she cried, opening the door.

To her surprise, Mr. Jams was packing.

He was sitting on an overstuffed and battered suitcase. His beard was tangled, there was jam on his nose, and his cheeks looked redder than dragon's fire.

Ooomph! Crash! The suitcase popped out from under him. Its contents spilled across the floor: maps and a book, shirts and socks, and even a jam jar. Mr. Jams landed with a thump beside it.

"Oh fairy-spitting ficklecorns!" he cried. "That's the third time!" His bushy eyebrows rose as he looked up at Clover. "So the egg moved, eh?"

"Yes. At least, I think so. Just a little, but . . ."

"Then there's really no time to delay. I'll go check on it, if you would be so kind as to try and close this blasted case. Maybe you will have better luck with it."

Clover gulped and hurried over, while Mr. Jams bumbled out of the room and down the hall.

A piece of toast, gooey with strawberry jam, lay on the desk, untouched. Cinnamon toast was his favorite, but strawberry jam was a close second. Mr. Jams never left toast of any kind uneaten. Something big was going on.

What could it be? she wondered as she neatly repacked his case. The maps were all unidentifiable to her. The book was Volume 15 of *The Magical Animal Encyclopedia: Nests and Shells.*

With the shirts folded, the book and maps on top, and the jam jar tucked between socks, there was plenty of room. When she closed the case, she noticed a dragon-shaped crest with the initials *T.J.* on it. *Those must be Mr. Jams's initials*, she thought. But what did the dragon mean? Did Mr. Jams belong to some sort of secret magical society? She'd never seen him use magic at the Agency, but there was definitely something special about him.

As she was doing up the clasps, Mr. Jams came back.

"Why, you are a miracle worker!" he exclaimed.

"Just organized," replied Clover.

"Is that all?" Mr. Jams chuckled. "Well, I'm glad to say that the egg shows no signs of hatching anytime soon. Even though we don't know what is inside of it, it is undeniably a spotted egg. When magic spotted eggs are ready to hatch, they make noises, wiggle and jiggle constantly, and their spots change color. None of these things has happened yet, thank the griffins. I need more time."

Mopping his forehead with his handkerchief, he collapsed onto the couch. Clover sat down beside him. Dipity wormed out from under the table and leapt up between them.

"Why?" Clover asked, tentatively. "Where are you going?"

"There's a magical animal expert who lives not too far from here, but studies in seclusion."

"An expert? On magical animals? Aren't *you* an expert?"

"At making cinnamon toast, perhaps." He chuckled again, then continued, "This expert is from a well-known wizard family, the Von Hoofs, who have studied magical animals for hundreds and hundreds of years."

"Oh . . ." Clover said. She supposed it made sense that you had to be from a magical family to be an expert on magical animals.

"His great-grandmother was founder of the Royal Claw and Tooth Society, his brother is curator of rare and fantastical relics at the Magical Animal Museum, and he himself is chief editor of the *Journal of Unusual*

Eggs and wrote three volumes of *The Magical Animal Encyclopedia*," Mr. Jams went on.

"Wow," said Clover. Not only were they magical, they all had impressive titles too.

"This expert's specialty is eggs. He can only be reached by foot. I must fetch him posthaste. He will be able to determine what is growing inside our egg so that we can be properly prepared."

"Can't we just wait until the egg hatches?"

Mr. Jams shook his head solemnly. "Ah, no. Then it will be too late to prepare. Baby magical animals often develop much more quickly than ordinary animals. They are rarely helpless at birth. Magic quickens growth, balance, and strength. What takes a non-magical creature weeks might take a magical one merely days. Even Dipity, you must have noticed, is growing quicker than a regular kitten, though perhaps not as quick as most magical kittens because of his encounter with the witch."

"Her potion didn't hurt him, did it?"

"No, no, but he might not have any magic ability beyond being green," said Mr. Jams.

"I don't care," said Clover stoutly. "He's magic enough for me."

Mr. Jams smiled. "Time will tell if he shows any

other magic. But we have no time to waste with the egg. What if it contains a rare merturtle that needs to be placed directly into the saltwater of the saltiest sea to survive? Or a nine-headed bird that needs nine times the food?"

"What about the formula the centaur delivered?" Clover asked. "There are lots of bottles of that."

"Nutrient Formula will do in a pinch, but it is certainly not as delicious as their natural diet. Unfortunately, Cedric couldn't fulfill my order for phoenix tears. What if the hatchling is some sort of unusual basilisk? A basilisk's bite is fatal, my dear, and the only antidote is those tears."

Clover gulped. She hadn't thought about that. A basilisk was a giant poisonous snake. If it was a basilisk, maybe her feelings toward it would change. Could she love a creature that could kill her?

"The journey shouldn't take me long," continued Mr. Jams. "I will be back three days from now at the latest."

"But, Mr. Jams—" started Clover.

"Now, now, I know last time I was gone longer than I said I would be. But this time I will be as punctual as possible. You are perfectly capable of looking after the Agency. You did it before and you can do it again."

"But—"

"There are plenty of supplies for the animals. I've made sure of that. And the gnome will take care of the place at night, as always."

"But—"

"And, just in case, I have left Dr. Nurtch's number on the desk. She is a good friend of mine and an outstanding magical animal veterinarian. But I feel certain nothing will happen."

Clover wasn't as sure. Last time so many things had gone wrong. But she *had* managed to take care of them in the end. She probably could this time too.

Mr. Jams pulled out his pocket watch.

"Oh, cripes and clawsnatch! Is that the time? I must be off. Don't forget to keep the egg surrounded with feathers and turn it twice a day. If you have a chance, you could do some follow-up calls. We should check to make sure the recent adoptions are going well. I'll be back in a fairy's twinkle." With that, he picked up his suitcase and headed out the door.

"Don't forget this," Clover cried, remembering the toast.

Mr. Jams took the piece with a smile. "How did I get by without you? You really *are* a miracle worker, my dear."

Clover blushed.

From the open door, she watched Mr. Jams walk down the path until he disappeared into the Woods.

Without thinking, Clover put her hand in her pocket, feeling for a lucky charm, forgetting for a moment that she had given those up. She couldn't rely on a charm anyway. She had to make her own luck.

3

A Colorful Cracking

Mr. Jams had told Clover not to worry about the egg. And the best cure for worrying, she knew, was to do something. That was a good thing about the Agency. There was always lots to do.

First she checked the egg. It wasn't wiggling or jiggling. It wasn't making noises. Its spots were the same. So, even though her stomach felt funny, after turning the egg carefully, she left it alone. After all, she was no expert.

And it was time to feed the animals—something she *did* know about. She prepared mush for the unicorns with a bit of cut-up apple, just the way they liked it, and found the spiciest dried peppers for the fire salamanders. After giving a sugar cube to the fairy horses and moon milk to Dipity, she lingered by Snort's old pen. She missed Snort, although feeding a dragon with fire-breathing problems had been very troublesome. Mr. Jams said to enjoy the calm while it lasted. New animals were bound to be brought in, sooner or later.

But the bell at the front desk announcing new customers did not ring that morning, so after breakfast Clover scrubbed the kitchen and swept the floors. She didn't like doing chores at home, but this was different. At home she never swept up unicorn hay or sparkles from princesses' dresses or a magic kitten's green fur. She made sure she got every one of Mr. Jams's toast crumbs (and some stray blobs of jam too). Then she organized the filing cabinet and dusted the Wish Book, a giant tome to record information about customers who didn't find the animal they were looking for.

When she was finished, she stood in the front room and admired her work. Then she pulled out a cheese-and-tomato sandwich and a postcard from her bag and sat down to take a quick break.

The postcard was from her best friend, Emma, who was away at Pony Camp for the summer. Clover hadn't had a chance to read it yet. There was a picture of a spotted horse on the front, and Emma's neat writing on the back:

Hi Clover,

Thanks for your postcard! Here is a picture of my horse Gracie—well, it isn't actually Gracie, but it looks just like her! We are going on trail rides every day. Everyone here loves horses just like me. Wish you were here too. You said that you had a job working with animals? Tell me more!

–XOXO, Emma

Clover nibbled at her sandwich and reread the postcard a few times. What could she write back?

She certainly couldn't say anything more about her job. She had to keep the Agency secret; she had promised

Mr. Jams. She probably shouldn't have even mentioned it to Emma in the first place, when she'd written earlier. She had just been so excited.

Her parents knew only slightly more—that she had a job at an animal adoption agency—but that was it. She was grateful that they were so busy with their own work at the mayor's office they didn't pester her for details.

But Emma was obviously more curious. Clover couldn't tell Emma anything else, as much as she might want to. Not about Mr. Jams, the egg, even Dipity. Mr. Jams said that most non-magic folk didn't know how to deal with the magical world and might cause trouble. And that was the last thing Clover wanted.

Of course, she *could* tell Emma that she wasn't unlucky anymore, that she had realized people make their own luck. But she couldn't tell her how she had discovered that either, since it had all happened at the Agency.

Clover tucked the postcard away. She would write to Emma later.

Instead, she picked up something else she had wanted to read: *Basilisks: Kings of the Serpents.* It was covered in sticky fingerprints. Mr. Jams had obviously read it a lot.

Snakes didn't scare her, but basilisks did. Luckily, the book said that baby basilisks spent the first few days

sleeping in their open eggshells with their eyes shut. And their glance wasn't deadly until they reached six months. But they *were* born with their full fangs.

"I'm glad you don't have poisonous fangs, Dipity," she said, pulling the cat onto her lap and giving him a pat. "Hey! What's this?" There were sticky bits of strawberry jam in Dipity's fur. She sighed. Mr. Jams really did get jam everywhere!

Dipity looked up at her with innocent green eyes.

"Nice try. But you know I have to give you a bath." Clover set aside the book.

She had yet to bathe any of the animals, but had brushed down the fairy horses with a toothbrush in the washing room. Tansy had a particularly tangled mane, and Clover had spent extra time with a toothpick getting it perfect. She headed to the washing room now, scooping Dipity up under her arm.

The washing room was beside the kitchen. It was a special room full of tubs of different sizes that hung from the ceiling like strange decorations. An assortment of scrubbers was strung up along the wall. Some were square, others round. One was as big as Clover's head. The soaps were lined up by the sink, each labeled. There was a thin scaly bar of soap that looked like a slice of tomato for dragons, a sparkly snowflake-shaped bar to clean the unicorns' horns, bubble-shaped soap for hippogriffs, and a speck of soap almost impossible to see—for "Mimimice," said the label on its container. Clover didn't know what mimimice were, but she

imagined they were the sort of creatures Dipity would like to chase.

Dipity was not in a chasing mood now. He was in a mewing mood—doing so at Clover reproachfully, as though he knew what was coming.

"It won't take long," said Clover, filling the sink with a few inches of warm water, then a dollop of Paw-Perfect shampoo. It took her a few tries to scoop Dipity up again, but finally she did, and lowered him into the sink. She half expected the water to turn green like his fur, but it didn't. Dipity just mewed miserably and struggled to jump out.

"Oh, come on, silly cat, it's for your own good," she said.

She was trying to scrub behind his ears to get at that jam when she heard something.

It was whinnying. Not just one whinny, but a chorus! Her grip loosened and Dipity squirmed free at once. He leapt out of the water and bounded out the door. Clover leapt up too, and hurried out of the washing room, ran down the hall, and burst into the stables. The unicorns were tossing their horns, eyes wide.

"Shhh, shhh," Clover hushed, trying to calm them, though her own heart was pounding. Something had spooked them. And then she saw the feathers, drifting down like snow.

The egg!

She raced toward the pen. Feathers were everywhere, no longer piled up in a mountain in the center. And the egg itself was gone!

But a second later she saw it—in a far corner, against the wall, half covered in fluff. It must have wiggled and jiggled out of the nest and tumbled all the way over there.

She opened the gate and waded through the feathers till she reached it. It wasn't the entire egg, though. It was only part of the shell. And the spots had changed. They weren't yellow and white anymore. They weren't there at all! Everything had happened as Mr. Jams said it would, but *much* faster. Except for the spots—they weren't supposed to disappear!

Clover picked up a smaller piece of the shell. It was gooey on the inside, coated with a slime that looked like drool. The egg had hatched. But where was the animal? If only Mr. Jams hadn't left!

At least it can't be a basilisk, she told herself. *It would still be sleeping in its shell.* With that calming thought, she walked carefully toward the nest to check it—and stepped on something buried under the feathers, something that quickly moved out of the way. At least she thought she did. And she thought she heard a scratching too. But when she searched through the feathers, she found nothing except her blanket and more pieces of the shell.

Clover swallowed hard. What had been in the egg? And what had happened to it? Maybe it crept out the open gate while she was examining the eggshell? Surely it couldn't have gone far.

Her heart still racing, she hurried out and began to check every pen, every stall. "Here, little one," she called out in what she hoped was her gentlest voice. "I won't hurt you." But the creature wasn't hiding in any of the empty pens or with any of the unicorns. She checked the whole Agency, from top to bottom, over and under everything. Even inside closed cupboards, which most creatures could never get into. But who knew what kind of animal this was, and what it could or couldn't do? The only loose animal she found was Dipity, lying on top of the fire salamanders' heated tank, drying off. "Did you see anything?" she asked him, but Dipity ignored her and licked a paw, still clearly annoyed about the bath.

Clover had just secured all the windows in the Agency so the creature couldn't escape, finishing with the ones in the kitchen, when the floor started to tremble.

BOOM! An earthquake shook the Agency. Clover gasped and braced herself against a wall.

BOOM! BOOM! BOOM!

No—it wasn't an earthquake.

It was knocking. Something was knocking on the roof. Something giant.

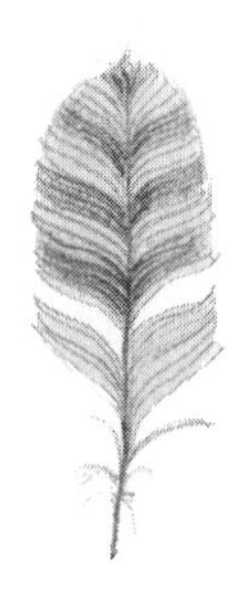

4

A Giant Request

BOOM! *BOOM! BOOM!*

The knocking shook the Agency again, and then a voice echoed, "Do you think it's closed?"

"No, no, my honey tub, there is a sign. It says . . . If I can only adjust my glasses. Yes, 'Enter,' so it must be open."

"Knock again, then, louder!"

Clover hurried to the front room. She didn't want the Agency to be knocked right over, or the hatchling scared half to death.

She opened the door a crack and peered out at the

largest, most perfectly manicured toenails she had ever seen.

She gulped and then stared up, up, up . . .

At giants! Two of the funniest-looking giants she could ever imagine.

Storybook giants were smelly and hairy, with yellow teeth and cracked nails. They wore dirty clothes and yelled "Fe fie fo fum!" Storybook giants were frightening.

These giants, on the other hand, looked about as terrifying as two tropical trees.

Maybe it was because of their clothes.

The lady giant was wearing an enormous flowery sundress, the straps stretched tight across her mountainous shoulders. A straw hat as big as a beach umbrella flopped on her head. She was in the middle of straightening it. The man giant was wearing a humongous Hawaiian shirt, shorts, sandals, and sunglasses, and a fanny pack the size of a small bathtub. If it weren't for their height, Clover would have thought they were people from her town who'd gotten lost in the Woods. But the giants were twenty feet tall—just taller than the peak of the Agency's roof. Clover didn't quite come up to their knees.

"We should have brought the sunscreen, Humphrey,"

said the lady giant to her companion. Her voice echoed down to Clover. "The sun is burning my shoulders."

"Don't fret, Prudence, my peach tree," replied the giant—Humphrey—beside her. "We won't be long, I promise. Now, where is that Mr. Jams?"

Clover took a deep breath, slipped outside, and closed the door cautiously behind her. "Mr. Jams isn't here," she shouted up to them. "But I am."

"Oh," Humphrey said, taking off his sunglasses, putting them in his pocket, and peering down at her. "And who are you?"

"My name is Clover. I work here at the Agency."

Prudence sniffed. She leaned over to Humphrey and whispered, "She is very tiny and I don't think she is from here. She's certainly not a witch or a princess. I think she's just an ordinary child. Why would Mr. Jams hire *her*? His cousin did a fine job of looking after the Agency before—full of spells to keep animals in line—and at least he's *local*."

"Why, I'm not sure, my winsome whale," replied Humphrey.

Clover, who had heard every word, wasn't sure either. Wouldn't someone from the Woods, or the magical lands beyond, have been a better choice? She didn't have any special abilities to keep the animals in line. Maybe if she could do spells, she could find the hatchling, but she wasn't magic, just like Prudence said.

"We will have to go someplace else," continued Prudence.

Humphrey whispered back, "But, my triple-layer cake, we've come all this way. Surely we should see if they have something here."

Clover mustered her courage. "Mr. Jams left me in charge while he's away," she shouted up at them. "What animal are you looking for? How can I help?"

Humphrey cleared his throat. "Our goose lays golden eggs and pesky thieves are always trying to steal them. We are gentle giants and unable to provide protection ourselves. We are in desperate need of a guard animal. But we don't want anything vicious, mind. We tried out my sister's pet griffin, but that was a nightmare." Here he pointed to a bandage the size of a bath towel on Prudence's arm and another just above his own knee.

Clover thought of the loose animal and how Mr. Jams had told her that not all pets were nice. She turned back to the Agency, checking to make sure she had firmly closed the door.

"Ahem," coughed Prudence.

Clover turned her attention back to the giants.

"I have, you see," continued Prudence, "the disposition of a kitten, soft and sweet. Isn't that true, Humphrey?"

"Quite so, my lamby flock," replied Humphrey.

"So we certainly don't want a dragon," said Prudence. "I've heard they can give dreadful burns. My skin is very delicate. And no phoenixes either, for the same reason."

"We don't have any dragons or phoenixes right now anyway," said Clover.

"Could we look around?" asked Humphrey.

"Well . . . you can't fit inside the Agency, but I guess I could open the back doors to the stables to let you look."

"Yes, that sounds like a fine plan," said Humphrey. "Doesn't it, my jumbo muffin?"

But then Clover thought of the loose animal. "Actually, I can't, because, well . . . it's hard to explain. You said you have a goose that lays golden eggs? Do they hatch golden geese?"

"Don't you know?" said Prudence with a sniff.

"*Everyone* in the magic world knows about golden eggs."

"Well, I . . ."

Prudence sniffed again. "Golden eggs most certainly do not hatch golden geese. They are filled with liquid gold. Why do you want to know?" She stared at Clover suspiciously.

"I . . . I . . ." Clover stammered. "I thought it might help to know what animal to suggest. I could bring a unicorn out front to show you, but—"

"A fine plan," said Humphrey again.

"But . . . honestly, I don't think a unicorn would be a good match. They aren't really meant to guard things."

"I knew it! All this way for nothing but a sunburn," moaned Prudence. "And our poor goose is sitting on a fresh clutch of eggs too. I bet some rascal is climbing up the beanstalk as we speak."

"There is *something* I can do for you," said Clover quickly. "I could write you down in the Wish Book, so when the right pet comes in, I can phone you."

"See, my pie pantry, that's not nothing," said Humphrey with a giant grin.

"The book's just inside," Clover said. "One moment."

She slipped back into the Agency, clicked the door shut right behind her, and lifted the book from its stand. It was so calm and quiet—no sign of a loose animal. Not even Dipity—he was probably still warming himself on the salamander tank. She hugged the book to her chest and was at the door before she realized she had forgotten a pencil. She hurriedly found one in the desk and went back outside.

Prudence was tapping her foot impatiently, causing the ground to tremble. It was hard to hold the pencil steady as Humphrey dictated.

"H-U-M-F-R-E?" asked Clover, who was never good at spelling.

"No, H-U-M-P-H-R-E-Y."

Prudence tapped her foot even harder, and the pencil slipped from Clover's fingers. She picked it up. "H-U-M-P-R-E-Y?"

"No, no!" said Prudence, stomping this time, and sending both the book and the pencil flying out of Clover's hands.

Clover's bottom lip quivered.

"There, there." Whether Humphrey was saying this to comfort Clover or Prudence was impossible to tell. "I brought a special pen just for situations like this." He fiddled with the zipper of his fanny pack and produced a pair of very thick spectacles that looked like two mammoth magnifying glasses glued side by side. He put them on. Then he took out an extremely long and thin pen and picked up the book, pinching it between two fingers. To him, it was the size of a postage stamp. Using the special pen, he began to write.

When he was done, he handed the book back to Clover. The letters were shaky, but legible, and glittered gold.

Humphrey and Prudence Butterbean / Castle Cliffs, #54 Beanstalk Way, 999-999-Eggs / Seeking a guard animal, gentle as a giant.

"Thank you," said Clover. "I never thought giants could write so small."

Humphrey smiled. "It's my invention, that ballpoint pen, actually, made with golden yolk ink."

"Humphrey, we must be on our way," interrupted Prudence. "We've already left our beanstalk unattended for far too long. With no guard animal, we will simply have to resort to Plan B."

"What's Plan B?" asked Clover.

"Setting traps for the thieves. Human traps, of course."

"I think you mean *humane* traps, my honey hive," Humphrey corrected.

"Of course," said Prudence.

"Oh," said Clover. "Well, I promise I'll call if a suitable animal comes in."

Seeming satisfied with that, the two giants shook her hand with their thumbs and forefingers, and headed off, stepping over the gate—and the gnome—in one stride as if they weren't even there. Clover could hear the giants' booming voices, though, even as they disappeared into the Woods.

"Such a tiny, unmagical thing to be looking after this place. If you ask me, if anyone needs looking after, it is her."

"Yes, my jelly-bean jar. But remember what your aunt Mildred says . . ."

What Aunt Mildred said, Clover never found out. Their voices had faded at last. But they had left Clover with an idea.

Maybe she could make a humane trap too, to catch the baby animal. It was a good idea, she thought—a giant one, after all.

5

Coco's Cold

Good ideas can take a long time to carry out. First, of course, Clover had to feed the animals supper. Then, after searching once more (just in case) for the missing hatchling, she got to work on the trap.

She started by mixing up a bowl of the Nutrient Formula. It was tricky to get all the powder to dissolve. She had to squish lumps of it on the side of the bowl with the back of a spoon. Dipity hopped up on the counter and looked over her shoulder, but didn't try to taste any. *Mr. Jams was right. It must taste pretty awful if Dipity won't eat it. I hope the baby animal isn't as picky.*

Clover carried the bowl of formula carefully to the egg pen. The animal was bound to go back to its nest sooner or later. Clearing a space free from feathers, she propped an old star-salmon crate up on a stick and put the bowl of formula underneath.

Once the trap was done, she shut Dipity in the room for small animals. He mewed unhappily, but she told him, "You never know, the hatchling might be small, but the egg was big, so it probably is too. You're safer here, Dipity."

Then she made a final round of the Agency, turning some lights on for the hatchling, so it wouldn't be scared. Even so, after she locked the door, she lingered on the top step, unwilling to leave, until at last she heard a *humph* from the gnome's direction.

She made her way down the path, stopping when she reached him.

"The egg hatched," she whispered, "and the animal is loose."

The gnome's mustache twitched.

"It's still in the Agency. At least, I think it is. I've

closed all the windows and locked the front and back doors, so it shouldn't be able to get out. I'm not sure what kind it is, but if you see an animal leaving that you've never seen come in, that would be it. Just keep a lookout, okay?"

The gnome's mustache twitched again, which Clover took for a yes.

She smiled. "Thanks."

By the time Clover got home, it was really late.

Luckily, her parents were still at work, but they had left Clover's favorite, macaroni and cheese, in the fridge. She ate three helpings, then flopped onto her bed and fell asleep in all her clothes, dreaming of eggs bobbing in the sky, wibbling and wobbling, about to hatch.

She woke up to eggs too. Her mom had made hard-boiled eggs and toast for breakfast. The eggs made her immediately think of the hatchling. "I'll eat later," she said. "There's something I want to check on."

"I'll pack an egg for you," said her mom.

"It's okay, Mom. There's lots to eat at the Agency."

"By the way," said her dad, looking up from his

plate, "we'll be late again tonight. Phone us if you need anything."

"I will," Clover said, though she knew she couldn't. The Agency had to stay a secret. Still, they meant well. She kissed them both good-bye and headed out the door.

The sun was beaming down on the Agency when Clover arrived. It was going to be another scorching day. *Hot as dragon's fire*, thought Clover, wiping her forehead.

Even the gnome looked hot. His mustache was drooping.

"Did you see anything?" she asked.

The gnome blinked.

"I'll take that as a no," said Clover. Then she added, "You should really be in the shade. You can move, now that I'm here."

The gnome didn't budge.

"But you have this," she said, patting his pointy hat, "so I guess you won't get sunburned. At least not on the top of your head."

The gnome blinked again.

"I wish it was easier to understand you. But I think you understand me, right?"

This time the gnome didn't blink. His eyes were shut—he was sound asleep.

Once inside, Clover plopped her bag down on the couch and hurried to the stables to check on the trap.

Even from outside the pen, she could see that the box had fallen. The stick lay toppled beside it.

The trap had worked!

Clover's heart pounded. She grabbed an empty oats bag from the tack room to scoop the creature into, then entered the pen. She crept toward the box, knelt down, and, moving as slowly as a fire salamander, lifted it with one hand. At last she would see the baby magic animal. . . .

It was . . .

Empty.

There was nothing in it at all.

Clover dropped the box and tossed down the bag. She stayed on her knees, staring at the floor in disappointment, listening to her own breathing. And then . . . she heard something sniffing. Something very close by. She held her breath, but she didn't hear the noise again. It must have been the baby animal!

Clover took heart. She couldn't really expect her first attempt to catch it to be successful. And at least now she knew the animal was definitely still inside the Agency. And all the formula had been lapped up, so it wasn't going hungry either.

It's too smart for that type of trap, thought Clover. *I need a better plan.*

She let Dipity out of the small animals' room and tried to think of something while she checked the Agency. There was no sign of the hatchling anywhere, but the unicorns seemed spooked, their ears back and their tails swishing. *Maybe they saw something*, she thought.

So, along with their morning mush, she gave them each a sugar-beet biscuit as a treat to calm them down, except for Coco, who had a sugar-beet allergy and got a crunchy carrot instead.

In fact, Clover gave all the animals treats. A thimbleful of applesauce for the fairy horses, who immediately pranced over to it, dipping their muzzles in, and a pepper stick for the fire salamanders, who poked their heads out from under their log, sniffing the air. For Dipity, she opened a tin of star salmon. He purred and rubbed up against her ankles, as though to say everything was forgiven for yesterday's bath and his night locked up.

Clover had just finished putting out another bowl of the formula in the pen, for when the hatchling was hungry again, and was feeling hungry herself now, when she heard a loud sneeze.

Achoo!

It was coming from Coco's stall.

Coco was the youngest of the unicorns, and named so because her mane and tail were a very light brown, instead of pure white like most unicorns. Even her horn was a dusty cinnamon color. Clover thought she was especially beautiful, but the princess who dropped her off last spring didn't. The princess wanted a different unicorn, all silver or gold, but Mr. Jams had refused to give one to her. "Princesses, pah!" he said with a humph when he was telling Clover the story. "All they care about is what glitters."

Well, Coco was certainly glittering now—from her nose.

The rims of Coco's nostrils were red, and from them dripped the strangest snot Clover had ever seen. It was sparkly! Coco's eyes, usually bright, were red and watery. Clover had been careful not to feed Coco a biscuit, so it couldn't be her allergy. And besides, this was all glittery. Maybe Coco was sick. Clover listened to the unicorn's breathing, but she wasn't wheezing or coughing. That was good.

Coco sniffled and looked at Clover woefully.

"Oh, you poor thing," said Clover. "I'll be right back. I'm going to get you some help."

She found the number Mr. Jams had left and phoned the vet, but only got a message. "You've reached Dr. Nettie Nurtch," said a gruff voice. "I'm either out on a call, or I've finally been stomped to death under the hooves of a hofflepoffer. Leave your name and number after the beep and I'll get back to you if I return alive."

Clover wasn't sure what to make of the message. She left a stammering reply, then hung up the phone—hoping the vet hadn't been trampled—and went into the kitchen to check the medicine cabinet.

On the UNICORN AND PEGASUS shelf there were bottles that read FEATHER GROWTH STIMULANT and HORN HELPER PILLS, and more of the sugar-beet biscuits. But nothing for a cold. So Clover grabbed a towel for the sparkles and went to rub all the glittery goo away. But it didn't help! More sparkly snot dribbled from Coco's nostrils, pooling on the floor in a diamond-bright puddle—and leaving glittery snot all over Clover's dress.

Clover wiped away what she could with the towel, then hurried back to the front room, planning to ring Dr. Nurtch again.

She knew someone was in the room before she reached it. The smell of strawberry cupcakes floated down the hall, making her stomach rumble. But she was surprised to find it wasn't just delicious smells that were floating in the Agency.

The new visitor was floating too, in the middle of the room, a foot above the floor.

He was floating because he wasn't a woodsman, a wizard, or even a giant.

He was a ghost.

A very rosy-looking ghost. Probably this was because of his big red apron. It covered most of his round body and was tied with a flourish around his large waist. A

long white mustache wisped down to the apron's pockets, like trails of whipped cream. From the pockets stuck spoons and spatulas. His cheeks were round too, but slightly transparent. Clover was surprised to see him holding a basket—could ghosts lift things? Clearly this one could. From the basket the most delicious smells drifted—not just strawberry but also vanilla and chocolate.

"Ooooo," he said. His voice had a whoosh to it, light as a breeze. "Perfect timing. I was just about to ring the bell. My name is Monsieur Puff."

"I'm Clover. What can I help you with?"

"It is this." Monsieur Puff opened his basket. Tiny cupcakes, small but perfect, began to float from the top. Before they drifted away, he gently pulled them back down and closed the basket lid.

"Cupcakes? They smell delicious," said Clover. "But this is an animal adoption agency, Monsieur."

"Yes, yes," replied Monsieur Puff. "My cupcakes are so fluffy they float, and so light they lift off the tongue. I knew they were delicious, but I didn't expect this kind of popularity. It all started with a Moonlight Picnic."

"A Moonlight Picnic?" puzzled Clover.

"Have you not heard of them? Moonlight Picnics—why, Midday ones too—are quite popular in the summer season—for magic folk, of course."

"Oh," said Clover. "Of course."

"I was supposed to deliver my usual frog-eye pies, but I ran out of frog eyes and made these lighter-than-air cupcakes instead. They were a hit! Why, even the ogres are ordering them now. I need help with my deliveries. My flying is not what it used to be, and I am quite exhausted. I was hoping to adopt a creature to help

me. Perhaps a winged horse? I have heard they are generally sweet in temperament and can fly like me."

"We don't have any winged horses at the moment," said Clover.

"What about a creature that floats?" asked Monsieur Puff.

Clover shook her head. "Sorry."

"One that has recently passed, perhaps? A ghost horse might be quite like a winged one, after all."

"Um, we don't have any dead animals here, Monsieur. Only living magical ones."

Monsieur Puff sagged. "I never had a pet, you know. Not even during my life. I was always too busy baking. I know food, but not animals. Maybe this was a . . . an undercooked idea of mine."

"I didn't mean YOU shouldn't have a pet—I just don't think there are pets that are ghosts. But . . . that doesn't mean there aren't good pets *for* ghosts," Clover said.

"I don't think so. . . ."

A loud *ACHOO!* interrupted him.

"Oh dear," said Clover. "One moment, please, Monsieur. I have to check on Coco."

"Cocoa?" He perked up at the name, floating a few inches higher. "Now *that* I understand. Cocoa, cinnamon, vanilla."

"Coco is one of our unicorns. But she is sick with a cold. Perhaps you should stay here. I don't want you to get sneezed on."

Monsieur Puff followed her anyway, after setting his basket on the desk. Clover noticed that a light dusting of flour trailed after him. She would have to clean it up later.

"Oh, you poor thing," she cried upon seeing the little unicorn. Rivers of sparkly snot flowed from Coco's nose. Clover picked up the towel she had left in the stall, but it was soaked through. "One second, Monsieur. I need a dry cloth. Please stay here."

Clover hurried to the washing room.

When she got there, she froze. In the center of the room, a cleaning bucket was toppled on its side. Rags streamed across the floor. One had been chewed to ribbons!

But there was no animal chewing on it now. No animal behind the counter or in the sink. Where could it be?

Was that sniffing again? She crouched down to listen, but heard nothing.

When she returned with a fresh towel, the ghost was inside Coco's stall, rubbing some snot between his wispy fingers, while Coco nosed his apron, probably looking for treats.

"Don't touch that," said Clover. "You might get sick too."

"Sick? No, no," said the ghost. "This little creature is not sick. She is allergic. All magic folk know that certain allergies cause sparkly snot."

"Oh," said Clover, blushing. "Well, I'm not magic. . . . But I do know about Coco's allergy. She's got a sugar-beet one. But I was really careful not to give her any of the sugar-beet biscuits this morning. Are you SURE this is an allergic reaction?"

"Entirely," replied Monsieur Puff. "I know allergies well. Why, half my customers are allergic to one thing or another. Most elves can't eat carrot cake. Fauns have a hard time digesting strawberries, so their cupcakes are always blueberry. And one little witch I know is so allergic to slugballs, she sneezes if they are even in the room."

"Well, there were lots of sugar-beet biscuits in the stables today. Maybe she was reacting to those? But the other unicorns have eaten them around her before without Coco having a problem."

"Allergies *can* worsen over time," said the ghost.

"She'll get better now that the biscuits are all gone, won't she?" said Clover.

Monsieur Puff nodded, but added, "She really shouldn't come in contact with anything made with sugar beets, though. I bake with cane sugar and honey myself."

That gave Clover an idea. Monsieur Puff knew about allergies. He would be able to keep Coco healthy, and Coco seemed to like him.

"You know, although unicorns can't fly or float, they are sweet in temperament, like winged horses," said Clover. "They're fast and light on their hooves. And they rise to the occasion when they're needed."

The ghost smiled. "Rise to the occasion—I like that," he said. "And I like Coco too. Yes, yes. I will make special treats, just for her."

To that, Clover smiled. Maybe she wasn't magic, but she still could make a good match.

After all the paperwork was filled out, Monsieur Puff left Clover one of the magic cupcakes—weighting it down by adding a gigantic jujube to the top that he pulled from his pocket—and a card in case she wanted to order more.

Then he floated away, leading Coco behind him. All that was left was a trail of hoofprints in the flour on the path, and heart prints inside Clover, who always felt sad to see an animal go. Sad, but this time, also inspired. The prints had given her an idea.

6

Dipity and the Disasters

Clover spent her last hour at the Agency sprinkling the floor with stardust. There was no flour but the stardust, used for shining the unicorns' horns, was a fine powder that glowed slightly. If the little loose animal stepped in it, it would leave footprints wherever it went. It was a perfect way to find it, Clover thought.

Luckily, they had lots of stardust, kept in the tack room in the stables, and Clover was sure Mr. Jams wouldn't miss a little. The bottles were hard to open, though, and every time she tugged out a stopper, a poof of the dust escaped.

When she was done, there was powder in her hair,

on her dress, even in her ears! Clover admired herself in the Agency's bathroom; her hair was glowing and her cheeks glittered. Her whole body twinkled like a star. But she knew she couldn't keep the dust on. She tried to brush as much off as possible. What she really needed, though, was a bath.

After checking the animals and locking up, she hurried home, hoping she wouldn't be spotted by the neighbors, and stuffed her dress under her mattress (she would wash it later). It would be hard to sleep if she was glowing, and even harder to explain to her parents.

Thankfully, they weren't home from work yet, so she filled the tub extra full and used her favorite bubble bath. She noticed that it smelled just like the floating cupcake she had brought home with her.

Clover eased herself into the warm water. As the magical stardust washed away, she felt a pang of longing. With the stardust on, she had felt sparkly—special, almost magic. Now just the soap bubbles twinkled. If only she really did have magic. If she were a fortune-teller, for instance, she'd be able to predict where the animal would be next. But then she thought of Miss Opal, who hadn't even been able to find her own pet. Maybe a fortune-teller's magic wouldn't work. But a witch's spells could surely help to find the animal. And even a princess had handmaidens who could search day and night. If only she weren't so ordinary . . . perhaps the hatchling would be safe and warm in a pen back at the Agency by now.

She worried about the little loose animal. Didn't most baby animals make noises? She was sure a baby dragon would grunt or roar, and a baby griffin would probably peep like an eaglet. But a magic salamander might be silent, so maybe some other creatures would be too. Her worries eased after the bath, when, clean and in her pajamas, she ate Monsieur Puff's cupcake before her spaghetti. It *was* delicious—like eating a cloud. That was a good thing about her parents working late. She could have dessert first.

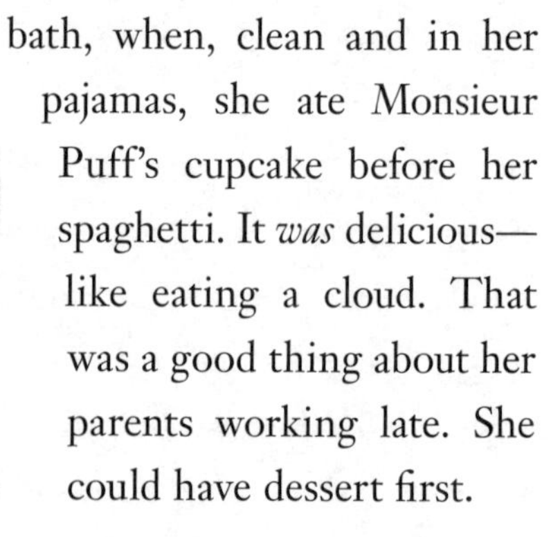

Clover knew something was wrong at the Agency the moment she noticed the gnome was not at the gate. He was standing beside the Agency's front door.

From the downward tilt of his mustache, she could tell he was not happy. Beside him stood none other than Cedric the centaur.

Cedric was wearing his blue cap, and a cluster of bags full of envelopes and boxes hung from his back. One box was sitting on the steps, near his hooves. There were holes in the lid, and it was taped and tied up in all directions. Silvery frost covered one corner and a black scorch mark another.

"I wish all my company was like you," Cedric was saying to the gnome, who was also standing on the front steps. "You can't imagine the princesses. They love to go on and on—and they are always ordering the most

awful stuff too. Once a perfume bottle burst in my bag and dripped onto my tail. I smelled like Strawberry Delight for a week—and let me tell you, it was NOT delightful."

Clover wondered how long the gnome had been listening to Cedric. The centaur *was* a talker. He waved upon seeing Clover.

"Hi, Cedric," she said. "Mr. Jams is away right now. Did you bring that for us?" She pointed to the box.

He glanced at it, and to her surprise, shook his head. "That was here when I arrived. No, no, I've brought some fresh feathers for the nest."

He handed her one of the bags from the bottom of the cluster.

"Thank you," she said—though feathers, fresh or old, weren't much use now that the egg had hatched.

"Well, I'd love to stay for some toast," said Cedric, "but I probably should get going. I've got to visit a sea queen today—and I need to meet her before the tides rise."

With a wave and a whinny, he was off, and Clover turned to the package.

"Where did this come from?" she asked the gnome.

The gnome, as usual, did not respond. But his mustache was still tilting downward.

"Do you know what's inside?" Staring at the frost and scorch marks, she added, "Is it dangerous?"

To her surprise, this time the gnome responded with a loud *mew*. Or at least, she thought he had. But when more mewing filled the air, she realized the noise was coming from the box.

It sounded just like Dipity. MANY Dipities! Clover had to see what was inside. She untied the twine, pulled off the tape with difficulty, and lifted the lid.

Inside, in a tangled heap, lay four fuzzy black creatures. They were very small, with itty-bitty pink noses and tiny twitching tails.

"Oh! Kittens!" exclaimed Clover. "They're so cute!"

However, when she reached in a hand to pet one, its orange eyes lit up bright blue. Out shot icicle-like beams, which sent an icy shock through her fingertips.

"Ouch!" she cried, pulling away her hand at once. The kitten blinked and his eyes turned orange again. But the tail of the kitten beside it was causing new trouble—sparks crackled from it, like lightning.

The third kitten was balancing on the tip of its tail like an acrobat, while the fourth kitten had started to float up, hovering at the top edge of the box like a mini

thundercloud, threatening to float away. She gently pushed the kitten down and shut the lid, reusing a piece of tape to hold the lid closed.

These weren't regular kittens, that was for certain. Clover examined the box, searching for a clue. She found something tucked underneath it—a piece of paper. She pulled the paper out and unfolded it:

TO THE GIRL AT THE AGENCY—

I WANTED TO GET RID OF THESE CREATURES BY OTHER MEANS, BUT MY CURSED CURSE WON'T LET ME. IT'S ALL YOUR FAULT. SO HERE. TAKE THEM.

The note was unsigned but Clover knew it must be from Ms. Wickity, the witch she had accidentally splashed with lucky potion and who could now cast only good spells. Clover felt happy about that as she pocketed the note. In a way, she had helped save these kittens.

I wonder what Dipity will think of them, she thought as she struggled to unlock the door with the box under one arm and the bag of feathers hanging from her shoulder.

When she finally got the door open, what she saw was a total surprise. There were no tracks on the floor. But that wasn't the surprising thing—there was no stardust either.

It was all on the ceiling!

Clover closed the door and the room glowed. The whole ceiling twinkled like the night sky crowded with stars.

She didn't know that stardust floated. Maybe it was attracted to the real stars at night? But how did Mr. Jams get it to stick to the unicorns' horns? She should have read up about it before dusting it everywhere.

It was going to be really hard to clean up. She couldn't reach the ceiling, even standing on a chair. And it was bound to be all over the stables' ceiling too, and that was even higher up. So much for her great idea.

As Clover scanned the room for any sign of the animal, she noticed some pamphlets that had been on the table were now on the floor, and when she went to put them back, she saw that the table leg was chewed.

The animal WAS in here! thought Clover. *So if the stardust had been on the floor, it would have worked!*

That made her feel better, and she picked up the box of kittens and carried it to the small animals' room. The two fire salamanders were asleep in their tank, and the fairy horses were asleep too, standing up in a huddle. Dipity was snoring under the table in his basket. He opened one eye, then shut it again. She put the feathers down and checked the cages.

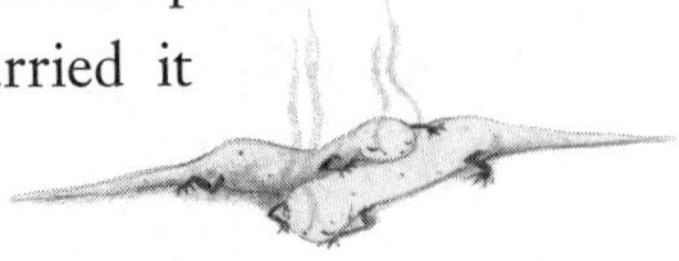

There were quite a few empty ones in the room. Only one, however, looked suitable for a litter of energetic kittens. It was very roomy, with a scratching post, a litter box, and bowls for water and food. She filled the bowls and then quickly moved the kittens one by one into the cage. The acrobatic kitten nearly flipped out of her hands, and the one with the sparking tail gave her a jolt that sent a tingle up her hand. She was relieved when she finally hooked the door shut.

Clover had never taken in any animals at the Agency, only adopted them out. Mr. Jams had mentioned checking them for diseases. She tried phoning Dr. Nurtch, but only got her answering machine again. What good was an emergency help number if it never provided help!

So, after feeding everyone breakfast, Clover decided to work on the kittens' card. All the other animals had cards that listed their names, species, age, and history. Clover had been looking forward to writing up the card for the animal inside the egg. But that would have to wait—right now she needed to focus on the kittens. The quicker she found them a home, the better.

She sat down at the desk in the front room and took out the quill pen. She had tried once to use the quill for paperwork, but ended up splattering ink on the front of her brand-new dress. Since then, she had watched carefully how Mr. Jams used it.

Clover dipped the tip of the quill into the inkwell.

She left the space beside *Name* blank to fill in later when the kittens were named. Beside *Species*, she put *Grimalkins*, proud of remembering that was the name for magic cats. The ink blobbed a bit on the *n* of *Grimalkin*, so it looked a little like an *o*. Unfortunately, quills didn't have erasers.

Age came next. Clover wasn't sure. She put *Kittens.* Now for the tricky part. *History.* She dabbed the tip of the quill in the inkwell again. It took a lot of thinking and scratching out to get it right.

> History: These ~~engergite~~ lively kittens were ~~abonded abanonded~~ left at the Agency and owned by ~~Ms. Wickity~~ a witch before coming here. Each has a ~~speshul~~ magic ability. If you have the time for an active kitten, ~~these guys girls kittens~~ one of these is for you.

Finally she was done. It was a bit messy, but she was certain it would look better when it was pinned up.

She was wrong.

It looked worse. The ink, still wet in places, trickled

down like tears. She had forgotten to blot it, like she had seen Mr. Jams do.

I'll have to redo it later, she thought, but first she needed to deal with the stardust. She had put that off long enough.

If she stood on a chair and held up a broom, the bristles just reached the dust. Slowly, she swept it into a corner of the ceiling, where it glowed softly like the last embers of a fire. The stables were much trickier because she had to stand on a ladder. It took all afternoon, and she couldn't get the dust that had floated above the unicorns' stalls. Her arms ached from lifting up the broom and she was completely worn out, but she still needed to figure out another way to find the hatchling.

Any chance of planning was interrupted by a crash from the small animals' room.

Clover hurried there, to find the kittens' cage door wide open and the kittens running wild. Or, more specifically—floating, tumbling, and zapping!

The kitten with the magic eyes was shooting blizzard beams at a table leg, causing frost to appear, while lightning tail played with the twisty-tumbling one. The

floating-cloud kitten, meanwhile, was hovering in the center of the room. The bag of feathers, which Clover had left there, was lying half-empty on the floor. The floating kitten's tail was sticking straight up and he was hissing—at her, it seemed. "Shh, shh," she said, trying to calm him down as she hurried over to scoop him up. Just then, there was a cracking sound.

She turned to see that the blizzard-beam kitten had caused frost to inch up the table leg, across the tabletop, and right to the salamanders' tank. The cold had caused the hot glass to crack.

"Oh no!" cried Clover. "Stop that!" she scolded blizzard beam, but he had already stopped—because the twisty-tumbling kitten had rolled right into him and now they were play-fighting. "Get back here!" Clover ordered, but, of course, they didn't listen. She examined the glass. The crack was only a hairline, but both salamanders were now huddled on top of their rock, sticking out their red tongues, which, Clover knew, meant they were frightened.

Lightning tail was staring at his reflection in an empty tank. A spark from his tail bounced off the glass, rebounded, and hit him in the nose, making him howl.

"Ahh!" cried Clover, running to get him. But the

instant she put her hands on him, his tail sparked and burned her skin.

"OUCH!" she exclaimed, letting go of him at once. Lightning tail bounded away to play with the others—who were all tumbling together in the feathers in the center of the room, even the floating one. "This is a disaster!" Clover groaned. *They* were disasters, little forces of nature. Blizzard, Cloudy, Twister, and Lightning. Those were the perfect names for them. If only she had a perfect way of dealing with them.

"I wish I was magic. Then I could—Dipity, no!" cried Clover.

Her green kitten had slipped out from under a table and was padding toward the playing kittens. He was clearly fascinated by them. His tail was twitching furiously. His ears too. Even his whiskers seemed alert.

"Silly cat!" Clover said, reaching down to pull him away—the last thing she wanted was for him to get hurt—and in that split second she heard purring. To her amazement, the four little kittens were asleep in a pile on the floor, like the calm after a storm.

Dipity mewed, pleased.

Clover seized the opportunity, ignoring her smarting hand, and scooped up the sleeping kittens one at a time, putting them in the cage. Then she fastened the door. Since she figured they must have been able to lift the simple latch, she hurried to the storage room to find a lock.

When she returned, Dipity was sitting regally beside the cage, staring at the kittens inside. They were still sleeping. Was it her imagination, or did the snores of the kittens seem to deepen the longer Dipity watched? Maybe Dipity did have a magical ability too, other than just being green. Mr. Jams said he might. Maybe he could calm other animals. Green *was* a calming color.

"Did you have something to do with this?" she wondered aloud.

Dipity just licked a paw.

Clover left him with the kittens to find a bandage for her hand, then checked the salamanders again—no heat was escaping from the crack in their tank, so she knew it was okay—and she checked the fairy horses as well, to make sure they weren't too startled. Some seemed extra rambunctious—Hickory was prancing around and around the tiny ferns—and Tansy, the gentlest, was trembling. Clover reached in and smoothed her miniature mane for a while to quiet the horse down. Then she cleaned

up the feathers and put them away in the stables.

Now, totally exhausted, Clover returned to the front room and slumped down on the couch. Her hand hurt. But her head hurt more.

Dipity mewed and pawed at her lap. "Not now, Dipity," Clover said.

But he mewed again, and Clover sighed and pulled him close. She rubbed behind his ears and he purred. It almost sounded like he was chuckling. Maybe he was. If those kittens hadn't been such a handful, it would've been funny. Especially when Lightning hit himself with his own spark. *A day of sparks and sparkling*, she thought, gazing at the ball of stardust twinkling up in the corner. "You probably knew it would float, didn't you?" she asked Dipity. But he didn't even twitch his tail. He was so relaxed. And so, she realized, was she. Her headache was gone.

Whether it was his magic working or not was impossible to tell. After all, it's hard not to feel better when you're cuddling with a kitten.

7
Tansy's Tantrum

It was a hot walk home, the air muggy. Clover took the shadiest route, which led her past Emma's house.

She glanced up at her friend's window. She still hadn't written back to Emma. Although Dipity was a good listener, she missed her best friend. Emma wouldn't be home till the end of summer. Mr. Jams, however, would be home tomorrow! Part of her wanted him back, but a bigger part was worried about what he'd think at the state of things. She wasn't the miracle worker he thought she was—he would see that now. If only she could come up with a foolproof plan to catch the hatchling. But how could she catch it when she still didn't even know what it was? The calmness she'd felt earlier, with Dipity, started to disappear. By the time she got home, she had a knot of worry in her stomach.

Her mom, home early for once, was making lemonade in the kitchen.

"Are you okay, Clover?" she asked.

Clover nodded, then, truthfully, shook her head. "Not really."

"What is it?"

"It's the Agency. I love it there, but I have so much to do. I don't know if I can manage it."

"You are the pluckiest girl I know," said her mom. "I'm sure you'll find a way." She handed Clover a tall glass of lemonade.

Clover took a big gulp. It was icy and delicious, and she felt a little better.

But the feeling didn't last. All night, Clover tossed and turned. It was so hot and humid she kept kicking off her covers, and in the morning, although there were clouds in the sky, it was hotter than ever. Her clothes stuck to her and her hair did too. She tied it up with her favorite ribbon, the one with four-leaf clovers on it.

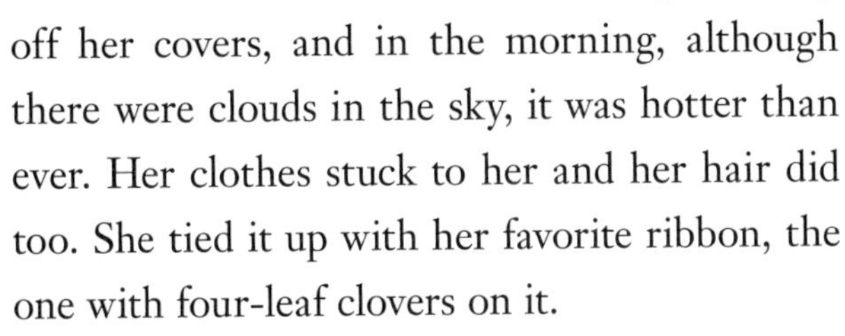

The inside of the Agency was roasting when she got there, and she wished she could open the windows to let a breeze through. But she couldn't risk the hatchling escaping.

The unicorns were all clearly bothered by the heat too. Clover made sure they had plenty of cool water in their buckets.

In the storage room, she dug out four fans from behind a stack of spare cages. She set up two in the stables and another in the small animals' room, for the kittens and fairy horses. (The fire salamanders, of course, didn't need a fan. They were happily sunbathing on their rock.) The last she set up in the front room, near the desk.

She sat beside it, trying to cool herself down and wondering what to do. She still had no new ideas for how to catch the animal. And the heat wasn't helping.

Then she remembered Mr. Jams's request. She could follow up on the adopted animals, to see how they were doing. She pulled out the files on Snort the dragon, Moondrop the unicorn, and Esmeralda (Flit) the toad, and took the phone down from the high shelf.

She tried Henry first. His mom answered. "Clover! Thanks for calling. Snort's settling in well. Henry's out with his Spell Scout troop right now. Snort is helping them roast hot dogs."

"That's great," said Clover. In Snort's file she put a check mark by *Follow-up call satisfactory*.

Next she tried Susie. No one picked up, but the answering machine message made her smile: "Olaf, Susie, and Moondrop are away from the phone at the moment. Leave a message after the tone."

Moondrop was clearly part of the family. She put a check in Moondrop's file too.

Next was Miss Opal. The phone rang a few times, and then a soft voice answered, "Miss Opal, your friendly fortune-teller here. What can I see for you?"

"Hi, Miss Opal. It's Clover from the Agency. I was just wondering how you and Flit are doing."

"Oh, dear girl! It is such a blessing to have Flit back. I was just thinking of you the other day. Is everything all right there? I had a terrible sense of trouble."

Miss Opal really was a good fortune-teller!

Clover didn't want to get into the problems with the hatchling, so she said quickly, "Don't worry, Miss Opal. Nothing bad's happened today." That was true, sort of.

But then, *CRASH!*

Clover jumped up and turned around. What was *that*? It had to be something in the room! Was it the animal? "Sorry, Miss Opal, but I've got to go."

"Do take care of yourself, dear. There's a storm coming."

"Thank you," hurried Clover, hanging up the phone and running around the desk. Would she see the animal at last?

But it wasn't the animal. Only the Wish Book.

Or what was left of it. One corner of the gilt cover was completely chewed up. Tattered pages were scattered around the floor.

Some chewed-up cleaning rags and a table leg were one thing, but this was another thing altogether! This was the MOST important book in the Agency.

"Now it's ruined!" Clover stomped her foot in frustration.

How had the animal gotten up to it? And why hadn't she noticed? Sure, she had been on the phone, but she was sitting only a few feet away.

She took a deep breath and picked up the Wish Book gingerly. The corner was dripping with drool. She gathered the loose papers together and carried the book to the washing room, where she carefully toweled it dry and tucked the pages back in their spots. Then she examined it again. It really was a mess. Luckily it seemed like most of the entries were readable, but the book itself was beyond repair.

Mr. Jams would be horrified. SHE was horrified. She took the book back to the front room and searched for other important objects that the animal might get at. She slid some pamphlets into a desk drawer, and was just putting the Wish Book away in the cupboard behind the desk when the bell rang. She turned around.

I hope it's not another new animal, thought Clover.

It wasn't a new animal. At least, it didn't appear to

be, for no creature accompanied the figure standing in front of the desk.

He was a very short man wearing a very tall, very green top hat. In fact, he was so short, all she could see from over the desk was the top of his forehead and the hat. Clover hurried around the desk to greet him properly.

The rest of him was dressed in shades of green too—a suit the color of freshly cut grass, shoes as green as watermelon rind, and a scarf that looked like a giant spinach leaf. Only his brown leather belt and the golden buckles on his shoes were not green.

"Are you a . . . a leprechaun?" she asked.

He laughed. "Yes, of course. Leonard Hue is my name," he said, shaking Clover's hand so hard her whole arm jiggled. "Is Mr. Jams here?"

"He's out at the moment. How can I help you?"

"Not me—my daughter. Come on out, Lulu."

A little face peeked from behind Leonard's stocky legs, then disappeared again. "Come on, Lu. Look—it's a nice girl who will help you find a pet."

Clover bent down. "Hello, Lulu. I'm Clover."

"She has a very lucky name, doesn't she, Lulu?" said Leonard.

Clover smiled as the little leprechaun girl shuffled

out and stared at her with big round eyes, magnified by the roundest, thickest glasses Clover had ever seen. The glasses took up half her face, and had sparkly rainbow-colored rims. Instead of wearing green like her father, the girl was an explosion of color. She was dressed in a multicolored tutu, which stuck straight out like a mushroom top, and a shirt striped like a peppermint stick. Her red hair was tied up on the top of her head in a messy ponytail, and tamed by a whole jungle's worth of animal-shaped barrettes.

Clover had never read anything about leprechaun girls before. In storybooks the leprechauns were always men and they always lived alone. But she had never read about ghosts that baked, or giants that used sunscreen either.

Lulu took off her glasses and began to polish them on her shirt.

"Lulu, please keep those on. You know you need them to see," said Leonard. He then added to Clover, "She just got them last week. It's been hard for her to adjust to them."

"How old are you, Lulu?" asked Clover.

Lulu held up one hand, her fingers and thumb spread wide.

"Wow! Five years old. I got my first pet when I was five too. A goldfish." (Of course, Clover didn't add that it had jumped down the drain the first time she cleaned its bowl.)

Lulu tugged on her father's sleeve and whispered something in his ear.

Leonard chuckled and tweaked her ear tenderly. "Those are just imaginary pets, Lu. Remember? We talked about this. Today we're getting you a *real* pet—no feathered fish or bunnies with antlers." Leonard turned to Clover. "She makes real snacks for them, you know."

Clover smiled. Even if they weren't real, feathered fish and bunnies with antlers sounded cute! And she probably would have made snacks for them too, when she was Lulu's age.

"Do you have any suggestions?" continued Leonard. "Nothing too big. She wants a unicorn, but I told her we'd get something smaller first, something easy to take care of."

"I know just the animal," Clover said. She turned back to Lulu, only to find that Lulu was peering under the desk, her glasses in her hand again.

"She must have dropped another barrette," Leonard explained, then said to Lulu, "Come here, Lu. Clover's talking about a pet for you."

Lulu stood up quickly and slipped her glasses back on as Clover explained.

"A fairy horse is kind of like a unicorn, but just the right size for you," she said. "Do you want to see?"

Lulu nodded again—so vigorously one of her barrettes popped off. Leonard shot out his hand quick as a toad's tongue and caught it in midair. "That happens a lot," he explained.

Clover led Leonard and Lulu out of the front room. Lulu glanced back.

"The fairy horses are just down the hall," said Clover. "In the small animals' room."

When she opened the door she spied, from the corner of her eye, that the kittens were up and at it again, and she hoped they wouldn't catch Lulu's eye as well. She was pretty sure a mischievous magic kitten wasn't what Leonard meant by "easy to take care of." Luckily, their cage was near the back of the room. And Lulu had her glasses off again, rubbing them on her shirt.

"Lu, your glasses," said her father with a sigh.

Lulu slid them back on.

"Look," said Clover, showing them the tank decorated like a mini forest.

Lulu adjusted her glasses and stepped forward.

The fairy horses were in different parts of the tank. Buttercup and Butternut were nibbling moss. Acorn and Hickory were snoozing standing up next to some tiny ferns. Tansy pranced up to the side of the glass and pressed her muzzle against it, right near Lulu's nose.

Lulu gasped and broke out in a big gap-toothed smile.

Clover pointed to the card beside the tank. "Mr. Jams rescued them from mean ogres who were mistreating them. Because they are so small, it's easy to make sure they get their exercise. And all they need are a few oat flakes or a bit of apple, and a nibble or two of a sugar cube for food."

Now it was Leonard's turn to nod vigorously. "Yes, just what I was hoping for! What do you think, Lu?"

Lulu smiled and pointed to Tansy, who was still standing next to the glass.

"That's Tansy," said Clover. Tansy was her favorite. Clover knew she probably shouldn't have favorites amongst the animals, but it was hard not to. More than the others, Tansy loved to prance around on her palm.

Clover remembered Mr. Jams's words: "Adoption is our Agency's purpose. It can be hard to part ways with our animals, but the Agency isn't a home for them. You will need to guard your heart, yet keep it open."

So she told Lulu the truth. "Tansy's actually my favorite because she is so gentle. She's a good choice. Would you like to hold her?"

Lulu nodded.

"Hold your palms out together, like this," said Clover, demonstrating. "Try to keep them as still and flat as possible. All she will probably do is nuzzle you or lick one of your fingers, but don't jerk your hands away. That might make her fall off and she could get hurt."

Lulu nodded again and held out her hands just as Clover had instructed. Clover carefully lifted Tansy out of the tank and placed her on the little leprechaun's palms.

"There you go, Tansy. This is Lulu. She might be adopting you."

Tansy sniffed Lulu's hands, then stiffened. And then . . . the gentlest fairy horse began to act like she never had before. She tossed her mane, reared up on her two back hoofs, and then began to buck furiously. Her nostrils flared and her ears lay back.

Lulu's lower lip trembled, and she looked up at Clover with frightened eyes, but she did not move her hands, though they were shaking.

"What's going on?" said Leonard.

"I . . . I . . . I . . ." Clover stammered. She wasn't sure herself, but she had to do something. She plucked Tansy from Lulu's palms.

As soon as Tansy was back in Clover's hands, the little horse quieted down. After a few snorts, she stood still.

Lulu pressed up against her father's leg.

"Are you okay?" asked Clover.

Lulu nodded slowly.

"That's my girl," said Leonard.

"You were so good," said Clover. "You didn't drop Tansy. You were brave and kept still. I don't know why Tansy acted like that. She's usually so gentle."

And now Tansy *was* gentle again, licking Clover's thumb.

Lulu tugged her dad's arm. He leaned over and she whispered something in his ear. Leonard smiled as he stood straight again.

"My daughter says that Tansy loves you so much she doesn't want to leave, and I think I agree with her. You did say that little horse was your favorite. You must take good care of the animals to have them so attached to you."

Clover blushed. "I don't know. . . ."

But she wondered if maybe he was right, at least about the attachment part, because when she tried to set Tansy back in the tank, the fairy horse didn't want to budge from her hand. She had to entice her off with a sugar cube.

When Clover was done, Lulu tugged on her arm and pointed to the tank again. "Oh, you want to try again?"

Lulu nodded hard. One of her barrettes popped off again and Leonard caught it.

"You *are* brave!" said Clover. "You must like animals as much as me."

Lulu smiled.

They settled on Hickory, a speckled fairy horse who especially liked to eat apples. "There are some wee apple trees near the Meadows where we live that are just the right size," said Leonard.

Hickory didn't make a fuss in Lulu's or Leonard's hands. And Clover even set up a makeshift paddock on the floor of the small animals' room, so Lulu could see how Hickory galloped. She laughed and clapped her hands.

With Hickory in a small carrying cage and the paperwork all filled out, Lulu and Leonard were about to leave, when Lulu spoke for the first time. "Can we take the puppy too?" She was holding her glasses again.

"Um . . . um . . ." Clover stammered, because, of course, they did not have a puppy.

"Now, now, Lulu, no more imaginary pets. You have Hickory. And do put on your glasses."

She did, then added softly, "Please?"

Leonard sighed, and with a wink at Clover, said to Lulu, "Very well."

Lulu looked at Clover too, as though to make sure.

Clover smiled. "Yes, of course you can."

"Come on, Lu," said Leonard. "We should hurry. It's looking stormy out."

And indeed it was. The sky outside the open door was now dark gray.

"It's about time for a storm. We're due for some rainbows. Rainbow Lane—that's where we live. You can visit us anytime, Clover. Thank you for all your help." He gave Lulu a little nudge to go.

"Thank you," Clover replied.

With a big smile, Lulu headed out the door after her father, holding Hickory's cage in one hand and her other hand in midair, resting on an imaginary puppy beside her.

8

Clover's Magic

The Agency felt quiet after the leprechauns left. The unicorns were unusually still, not even swishing their tails. The magic kittens were also acting oddly—not sleeping or bounding around their cage, but instead sitting perfectly in a row (except for Twister, who was standing on his head). A single spark sputtered from Lightning's tail, and Blizzard's eyes were flashing, but no beams shot out. Cloudy bobbed an inch above the bottom of the cage.

Maybe it's the coming storm, thought Clover. Indeed, the Agency was starting to cool down as clouds covered the sky, and so she put away the fans.

Still, she wasn't sure if it was *just* the storm. Something was different about the Agency. There was a new emptiness, a silence that hadn't been there before. Even Dipity was acting strange, keeping watch at the front door, his tail bristled, his ears pricked.

But Clover didn't realize what it was until the rain starting pattering down on the Agency roof, and she took an umbrella out to the gnome.

He wasn't just in a different spot, he was in a different position too. He was standing in the middle of the open gate, one arm raised and pointing down the path that led to the Woods. In the dust, which was slowly being speckled by the rain, Clover could see Leonard's and Lulu's footprints. And some other prints too. Some paw prints! They looked just like a puppy's!

Right away, Clover knew. She had asked the gnome

to watch out for the creature from the egg. She had asked him to alert her if it left. And it had! But it hadn't escaped through a window or a door. Lulu had taken it with her. She had taken the little animal that hatched from the egg, the little animal that Clover hadn't seen in the pen, or the trap, or anywhere, because of one simple fact.

It wasn't imaginary.

It was *invisible.*

That's why she couldn't find it! That's why the shell had seemed to be empty—and the trap too. That's how the Wish Book was destroyed right under her nose! And that's why Mr. Jams couldn't figure out what the hatchling might be! Clover had never heard of an invisible puppy before. In fact, Clover had never heard of invisible animals at all! She was tingling, she was so excited.

But Clover had let the puppy leave with Lulu . . . let him escape! She had to get him back.

"Oh, thank you, Gnome. Thank you!" She popped the umbrella over him, then raced back inside. There was no time to lose.

Leonard had told her they lived on Rainbow Lane. She checked Hickory's file to find out the house number:

#7 RAINBOW LANE, THE MEADOWS

There's a sign in the Woods that points to the Meadows, thought Clover. *That should lead me there.*

After digging out another umbrella from the storage room and making sure that everything, including the animals, was safe and secure, she found a small leash in the tack room, then searched the kitchen for a treat that a puppy might like. Regular puppies, she knew, would still be drinking milk, but regular puppies didn't hatch from eggs. She saw a bin in the cupboard labeled THREE-HEADED-DOG BISCUITS, which was filled with bone-shaped treats in three different flavors (goose, pheasant, and potato). With one of each in her pocket, she was about to leave, when a flash lit up the front room, and a moment later she heard a terrible *CRACK*, like a giant firework exploding.

She jumped. *A thunderstorm*, thought Clover with a shudder. She didn't like thunderstorms. She never had. When she was little, she'd hidden under the bed. She wasn't quite so scared of them now but still her heart was pounding. Thunderstorm or not, though, she had to get the puppy back. But her feet wouldn't move.

Mew?

She heard Dipity close by, then felt his tail brush her

legs. She looked down at him as he wove a figure eight around her.

"Not now, Dipity," she said.

There was another flash, followed by an even louder *CRACK!* Clover jumped, but this time she didn't feel scared. She really didn't! "Dipity, you calmed me. That *must* be your magic." She bent down and gave him a hug.

She opened the door, and he started to follow her. "You can't come with me, but I'll be okay. Thanks."

Dipity's tail curved like a sideways smile.

She smiled back at him, then shut the Agency door and turned the ENTER sign to CLOSED (EVEN FOR ROYALTY!). As she popped open the umbrella, she noticed that it had a bite taken out of it, a bite far bigger than a puppy's. It wouldn't provide much protection, but she shouldered it bravely and trudged forth.

The gnome was back in his usual position beside the gate, except the hand that had been pointing down the path was now holding his umbrella (unbitten, Clover noticed). Rain fell steadily, and she could see his boots were already splashed with mud.

"Can you watch the Agency for me?" she asked.

The gnome blinked.

“Thank you. I’ve locked the door. I won’t be gone long, I hope.”

Then she headed off, walking as fast as she could, with a quick glance back at the Agency, which was, as always, slightly lopsided, covered in vines, and, most of all, full of surprises.

Every day when she left the Agency, Clover followed the same path from Dragon’s Tail Lane through the Woods and out to her village, and had only ventured from it once, when she rescued Dipity from Ms. Wickity. Although it hadn’t been so long ago—just a few weeks—it felt like months had passed.

As she reached the signpost and the arrow that

pointed to the Meadows, she suddenly wished that she had asked Mr. Jams for a map or a tour of the Woods and Beyond. What if the Meadows was a long way away?

But Leonard and Lulu had walked, hadn't they? So it couldn't be too far. Or so she hoped. Already, the chewed-up umbrella was proving useless—her hair was drenched. The trees did little to stop the heavy rain, and the wind had picked up, sending small twigs and leaves skittering about like mice. Even though the thunder crashed, she stayed calm. Thoughts of the puppy kept her going.

She saw a man dressed all in green, like Leonard, with a golden umbrella, hurrying down the path.

He must be a leprechaun too, thought Clover. "Excuse me," she said. "Is this the way to Rainbow Lane?"

"If you have to ask, I can't tell you," he said, glancing briefly up from under his umbrella, then continuing on his way.

Clover trudged on.

Before long, she came to a sign that said, RAINBOW LANE, HOUSES 1–50, THIS WAY. And indeed, around the bend, the path grew wider and the trees thinned, opening up to a neat semicircle of houses that reminded Clover of little golden pots. The rain pinged noisily off their metal roofs, and the wind tore at their gates and shutters and nearly ripped the umbrella from her hand.

Beyond the houses stretched a sea of green grass, whipped by the wind. The Meadows. Boulders dotted the landscape, half-hidden in grass and mist. It was the perfect place for unicorns to roam, and Clover wondered if there were any unicorns that lived in the wild. Mr. Jams had once told her about wild dragons, but not wild unicorns. She would have to ask him sometime. But first—#7 Rainbow Lane.

Number 7 was the merriest-looking of the houses, with a crooked chimney and bright green shutters that seemed to be smiling despite the storm. Clover's heart was pounding again—but this time with excitement. In moments, she would finally meet the little animal that had hatched out of the egg. She knocked on the tiny door.

"Who is it?" came an unfamiliar voice from inside.

"It's Clover, from the Magical Animal Adoption Agency. I'm looking for Leonard and Lulu."

"Oh . . ." The door clicked and opened to reveal a plump and pretty woman dressed in a light green dress with a green apron and green slippers. Her eyes were amber-gold, like candlelight, the kind of eyes that made you feel warm inside.

"Oh dear, you're soaked. Come in, come in. Leonard and Lulu told me all about you. I'm Marigold, Lulu's mom."

Clover closed her umbrella and ducked, dripping, into the most cozy, colorful living room she had ever seen. Each wall was painted in a different vibrant color. So too was each cushion and chair a different hue. It was like walking into a rainbow. As she watched, she saw that one of the walls was slowly fading into another color.

Marigold saw her surprise. "It's rainbow-made paint. Rainbows are full of such amazing magic, aren't they? We haven't had any rainbows for a long time. Thank the skies for this storm—though I wish it wasn't so strong. Poor Leonard. He's out right now, harvesting."

"Harvesting . . . ?"

"Harvesting the rainbows, of course," said Marigold. "He'll be out for a while. I'm sorry."

Although Clover was curious about how rainbows were harvested, she replied, "That's okay. Really it's Lulu I need to speak to."

"I'm afraid she is a little upset right now," said Marigold. "But let me get her. She's with her new fairy horse. Just make yourself at home. Don't worry that you're damp."

While Marigold hurried out of the living room, Clover looked around. She couldn't see any sign of a puppy—but, of course, that was part of the problem. Marigold emerged a few moments later with a very sad-looking Lulu.

"Hush now," Marigold was saying to Lulu. "I told you that it's not real. Papa told you too." Then to Clover she said, "Sit down, sit down! Can I fetch you some tea? Or hot chocolate?"

"Hot chocolate, please," said Clover, taking a seat on the couch, which was slowly changing from red to orange.

Marigold bustled off to the kitchen, and Lulu sat down next to Clover. Close up, Clover could see Lulu's glasses were all wet, and tears streaked down her cheeks.

"Are you okay?"

Lulu sniffled. She took off her glasses and wiped

them, then looked across the room and smiled briefly before replacing them. Clover wondered if that's where the puppy was. But she couldn't see anything.

A knot formed in Clover's stomach. She HAD let Lulu adopt the puppy. What if Lulu was upset because she knew Clover would come back for it? Clover could easily imagine how awful it would be to get a new pet and then have to give it up right away.

"Lulu," she started in her gentlest voice, "I'm here about the puppy. It wasn't ready for adoption yet. I made a mistake. We didn't get a chance to fill out the paperwork or anything. I need to . . . to take it back."

Lulu shook her head.

"It's still really little, just a baby," Clover tried to explain. "You can come later and adopt it if you want, if your parents say it's okay. In fact, I think you would be a great owner. But right now, will you show me where it is?"

Lulu shook her head even harder.

"Please, Lulu. It's really important. I promise that you can come later and adopt it if you want. Please show it to me."

"He's gone!" wailed Lulu, just as her mom entered with a tray of steaming cocoa.

"Now, Lulu! I told you, no more about that puppy." Marigold turned to Clover. "I am so sorry. It's Lulu's imaginary puppy. Lulu insists that it ran out into the Meadows when it heard the thunder because it was scared. I've tried to tell her not to worry." Marigold sighed. "Lulu's always seeing things that no one else can. I wish I had as vivid an imagination."

"Actually it's not just in her imagination," Clover began.

Marigold looked confused. "What do you mean?"

"I mean that . . ." But Clover saw Lulu shaking her head and pointing outside.

Clover understood—it would take too long to explain everything; the puppy needed them. "I'll have to tell you later," she said. "Right now I have to find the puppy and I could really use Lulu's help. Could she come with me? I'll take good care of her."

Boom! Thunder crashed.

Marigold jumped, the cups rattling. She set the tray down on the table. "The storm is far too fierce for chasing a puppy, whether it's real or not. Even experienced rainbow harvesters like Leonard are going to be having a tough time. Why don't you stay for a nice cup of cocoa, dear, until the sun comes out?"

"I can't," said Clover. "I really must find the puppy. And Lulu's the only one who can help me."

Lulu looked hopefully at her mother.

But Marigold shook her head. "I'm sorry," she said.

Lulu's lower lip began to tremble.

"Don't worry, Lulu. I'll find him. I promise." Clover stood up.

"Oh dear, dear," sighed Marigold. "Well, if you must go out, then you should take this." Marigold handed Clover a rainbow-colored umbrella. "Yours looks like it has seen better days."

"Thank you," said Clover, taking it. She was about to leave when she thought of something. "Lulu, what's his name?"

"Just puppy," said Lulu. "I haven't named him yet."

The storm was a monster now—thunder rumbling, wind screeching. At least Marigold's bright umbrella, although small, was keeping Clover dry, unlike the other one. The minute she stepped off the path and into the muddy Meadows, however, her shoes were soaked. The

Meadows looked like the sea, and felt like it too: wet and endless. For all she knew, the puppy might be right in front of her. Far in the distance, through the mist, she could see a wall, rising like a swell on the horizon.

"Puppy! Here, Puppy," she called.

Clover whistled as loudly as she could above the wind. She reached out her hand, hoping to feel him. She even squinted her eyes, hoping she might see *something*. But she didn't.

She kept going. Around the boulders, through the grass. She came to a particularly marshy section and tried looking for paw prints in the mud, but if there were any, the rain had already washed them away.

"Puppy! Puppy! Here, Puppy!" she called until her voice was hoarse, but the wind drowned her out.

She trudged on, sinking down in the mud, nearly losing a shoe. She had just rescued it when the wind snatched Marigold's umbrella from her hand, flinging it away in a swirl of colors, up, up, and out of sight. It wasn't even hers to lose. Within seconds, she was truly soaked.

Her thin summer dress clung to her body and her shoes made slurpy sounds. Her hair was blowing into her eyes and she wiped it away, forgetting that her hand was covered in mud from pulling her shoe out of the muck. Now there was mud in her hair and on her face.

"PUPPY! HERE, PUPPY!" she called desperately.

Boom! replied the storm.

At last, Clover reached the crumbling stone wall at the end of the Meadows. It was only slightly taller than her, but still high enough to block her view of what lay beyond, and stretched as far as the eye could see to the right and the left. The wall was too high for a puppy to get over. But it did provide some shelter from the wind. Maybe the puppy was huddled up against it?

FLASH—a bolt of lightning lit up a hole between some of the stones. It was just big enough for a large puppy—or a small girl.

Clover squeezed through, though the last bit was tight. Puffing, she emerged to a terrible sight. The wall didn't mark the end of the Meadows!

Below her, stretching out for as far as she could see, were *more* Meadows, ten times larger than where she'd already been, with trees and boulders and grass. She would *never* be able to search it all. She would never find the puppy—even if she *could* see him!

CRACK! A zigzagging bolt of lightning struck one of the trees in the distance. The tree fell over with a sickening crash. Clover jolted and tripped over a rock. She tried to catch her balance, but slipped and slid down the slope into the Meadows.

"OH!" she cried. Down, down, down until—*THUMP!* She landed at the bottom, in a muddy, miserable heap.

She felt very alone, and very scared. If only she had Lulu's magic to see the invisible puppy. If only she had magic of any sort! Suddenly, all she wanted was her parents, a warm bath, and Dipity on her lap. Tears filled her eyes.

She got up and stumbled to some nearby boulders. Two leaned together, forming a little cave. She crawled into the dry space, wet and trembling.

She thought of the puppy, how he too must be wet and trembling. She imagined him curled up in a little ball, shivering and scared.

If she couldn't find him, if she gave up, would he die?

The thought was too horrible. Clover began to cry harder. It was hopeless—ridiculous, really—searching for something that you can't even see. She *should* just give up!

But she couldn't.

She wasn't magic, but maybe she didn't need to be.

Maybe it didn't matter. What really mattered was that she loved the magic animals, so she would never give up. Even when things were tough. And things *did* get tough. Like right now.

But she had figured out Dipity's magic and found homes for Coco and Hickory. A litter of kittens was safe and sound because of her. A fairy horse loved her so much that it didn't want to be adopted. She *would* find the lost puppy. She felt it in her heart.

And just as she felt it in her heart, that's when she felt it beside her too. . . .

9

Sense, Not Spells

There was something in the dry space in front of Clover. She could feel the heat from its body. And when she listened very hard, she could hear soft whimpering too.

But she couldn't see anything.

She reached out her hand—slowly, hopefully—and touched wet fur, but only for a moment. The creature quickly pulled away.

Clover gasped. It had to be the puppy!

He clearly wasn't like most puppies, not loud and barking. She remembered stepping on something in the pen. . . . Had it been his tail? She'd probably scared him. And then the big booms, the knocking of the giants, those must have scared him too. *He must be shy, just like Lulu*, thought Clover.

"It's okay," she said softly. "It's just a storm. Don't worry. I'm here to help you."

Clover remembered the treats she had brought and pulled one out. It was soggy, but it was better than nothing.

"Here, look. For you," she said, holding it out, hoping it was in front of him.

She heard the puppy sniff (very softly again—he was almost as hard to hear as he was to see) and all of a sudden an invisible tongue licked the treat out of her hand.

Clover heard some soft munching and saw some crumbs, and shifted closer, reaching out her hand again. This time the puppy flinched, but didn't shy away. Carefully, she petted him.

He certainly didn't *feel* invisible. He was very tiny and very wet. But even so, she could feel two floppy puppy-like ears and a wet puppy-like nose. He even had a puppy-like tail, which thumped softly on her shoe. As she felt down his back, she gasped. Something feathery and delicate was folded up near his shoulders: two very un-puppy-like wings, which trembled with every breath he took. He wasn't just an invisible puppy—he was a *winged* puppy, too!

That's how he reached the Wish Book, thought Clover. At least now she could explain what happened to Mr. Jams. Surely he'd understand. After all, it was hard to be mad at an invisible winged puppy!

She fed the puppy another soggy treat, which he gobbled up eagerly.

Clover had to get the puppy back to the Agency, dry him off, and give him a proper meal. The rain was still pouring outside of their shelter. They could try and wait out the storm, but who knew how long it might last? It was best to leave now. Clover reached for the leash in her pocket but realized that, in her hurry, she'd forgotten a collar. She'd have to carry him.

She reached to pick up the puppy, but with a whimper, he backed away.

"It's okay," Clover said again, crawling toward him. She took the last biscuit from her pocket and held it out. He gobbled it up, then licked her hand, as if looking for more.

"I'm sorry. That's it," she said. "But there are more treats at the Agency. Would you like to come with me?"

He licked her hand again.

"Good," said Clover. "But I need to pick you up, okay?" Slowly, Clover tried again. She slipped her arms under him, murmuring more words of encouragement all the while. This time he didn't back away.

Nestled in her arms, he seemed even smaller. She could feel his little heart beating next to hers. She sat like that for a moment, holding him tight. Every time the thunder rumbled, the puppy's heart raced. "Shhh, shhh," comforted Clover. "Nothing will hurt you. But we have to leave here, okay? Remember the treats?" The puppy licked her arm. "Let's go and get some."

And so, with the puppy tucked in her arms, Clover crawled out of the shelter of the boulders and headed into the storm and the muck of the Meadows.

Although it was still raining, inside she was beaming, happy and bright like the sun.

On the way back, Clover paused as she passed Lulu's house to show her that the puppy was safe. And sure enough, Lulu was pressed against the window. When she saw Clover and the puppy, she broke into a big grin and waved furiously. Hickory was perched on the windowsill. But Lulu seemed to be holding something in her arms too. Could it be one of her invisible animals? Clover remembered what Leonard had said—a feathered fish, a bunny with antlers. And what else might she have? Possibilities blossomed in Clover's imagination.

She noticed Lulu's glasses were sitting on top of Hickory's cage. She remembered all the times Lulu had taken them off at the Agency and how many times Leonard had said, "You can't see anything without them."

He was wrong, thought Clover with a smile. *Lulu can see lots without them.* Clover decided she would have to visit Lulu again soon, and meet all of her animals. She waved good-bye and hurried on.

By the time she reached the MEADOWS signpost, the storm had calmed down and so too had the puppy. He was no longer trembling, but instead wiggling—wiggling so enthusiastically, in fact, that he almost slipped right out of Clover's arms!

She wished she had a collar for the leash! Then she had an idea and sat down by the side of the path, with the wiggling puppy in her lap. She pulled off her hair ribbon and, with difficulty, tied it around the puppy's neck. It was extra tricky since she couldn't see where his neck was. Once the ribbon was secured, she clipped the leash to it. The ribbon did the job, and Clover let the puppy go, watching the ribbon bounce along, just above the path.

And then suddenly there was a tug on the leash as the ribbon floated up high—as high as the first branches of the trees. Clover gasped. He couldn't stay airborne for very long—after all, he was only a puppy—and dropped to the ground. But then he flew again. Clover watched as the ribbon rose up and down as though it were moving along a teeter-totter, all the way back to the Agency.

The gnome stood at the front door with his arms crossed.

Clover patted his hat. "Good job," she said. "I could never have found this puppy without you."

Then the gnome did something he had never done before. He mumbled! Clover was sure he said, "Gump."

"You CAN talk!" she said, surprised. "Gump—is that your name?"

But the gnome just blinked.

Clover smiled. "Gump. I like that. It suits you."

After making sure the puppy was dry and fed, Clover decided she needed to dry off too.

She took off her soggy dress in the washing room and, after a quick wash, wrapped herself in a big clean towel. She scrubbed as much of the mud from her dress as she could, then laid it over a corner of the salamanders' tank.

She was waiting for her dress to "bake," watching the kittens play, when the phone rang. Clutching the towel around her tightly, she hurried to the front room.

"Hello, the Magical Animal Adoption Agency. Clover speaking," she said.

"Oh, the new girl," replied a gruff voice. "Dr. Nurtch here. You called about a sick unicorn? Wish I could've called sooner, but I had a dragon with a bad case of dunglehop to deal with. And then a poor hippogriff whose owner tried to fix his split claw with a spell. A complete disaster! Sense, not spells—and care, of course—that's what I tell folks. But do they listen? No, of course not. So, about your unicorn . . . ?"

"O-Oh," stammered Clover. "Coco is fine now. She just had an allergic reaction. Sorry to bother you."

"Took care of it yourself, did you? Well, Mr. Jams did say you were a keeper."

"He did?" Clover couldn't believe it. A keeper! Mr. Jams thought she was a keeper. Clover was so surprised she almost forgot to ask about the kittens. "Oh, one more thing," she added. "We also got in a litter of magic kittens that needs to be examined."

"Ah, a new batch of kits, eh? I can soar by tomorrow to check them out. Does that work?"

"Yes," said Clover. "Mr. Jams should be back then too."

"Good, good. He does make a mean piece of cinnamon toast. Magic folk often rely too much on wands, when a simple toaster does the job best." There was a loud bleating in the background. "Well, must be off. Sense, not spells. Remember that, Clover."

And with that, Dr. Nurtch hung up, leaving Clover

rather befuddled, but very happy. Mr. Jams said she was a "keeper." Sense, not spells. That was her.

As Clover changed into her dry dress, she felt tingly warm, inside and out.

In the front room, the puppy and Dipity were curled up together on the couch—well, it looked like Dipity was sitting next to a floating ribbon—and the sun was shining through the window. Clover opened it a crack to let in a breeze. So many wonderful things had happened that day, so many mysteries had been solved. She wanted to share it all with someone.

There *was* one person.

Of course, she couldn't tell Emma exactly what she had discovered at the Agency, but she could tell her exactly what she had discovered about herself.

She sat down and pulled out a piece of paper from the desk. She still had to rewrite the card for the kittens, and now she could do one for the puppy too, but first she wanted to write to her friend. She took out the quill pen. She knew it would be messy, but she didn't mind. Emma would like that she had written with a real quill pen. And this time, Clover would remember to blot the ink.

Hi Emma,

I miss you too. Guess what? I haven't lost any animals so far. Instead I found one that was lost! Can you believe it? I'm actually good with animals after all!

–XOXO, Clover

P.S. I'm using a real quill pen!

By the time she was finished with the letter and the cards, more than a breeze was drifting in through the open window. The delicious smell of chocolate cupcakes was, too.

10

The Perfect Picnic

Clover watched through the window in the front room as Monsieur Puff floated up Dragon's Tail Lane. Sunbeams streamed through his body. Beside him trotted Coco. On her back, she balanced a large wicker basket.

Clover scooped up the puppy and opened the door, greeting Monsieur Puff as he came up the path.

"Clover!" exclaimed Monsieur Puff. "Just the person I wanted to see."

"What can I help you with? Is there a problem with Coco?"

"Nothing—no, no. You have already helped me

enough. You provided me with the most—how shall I say?—divine of pets. Why, it has only been two days, and already I can't imagine what I would do without her." Monsieur Puff rubbed Coco's nose, and the unicorn swished her tail proudly.

"With Coco's help, I have been able to make three times as many deliveries, and never does the basket tip or wobble. She trots as though she were floating. Why, I never imagined a pet would be such a . . . sunny-side-up experience. I wanted to thank you with some cupcakes." He began to unfasten the wicker basket from Coco's back.

"I've never gotten a thank-you gift before . . ." Clover answered, amazed, but before she could say more, the puppy squirmed in her arms.

"Now, what is that, my dear? I can't see it properly, but you are holding something, aren't you?" said Monsieur Puff, staring at the floating ribbon.

"It's a puppy. He's invisible." Clover let him jump down, and he bounded toward Monsieur Puff.

"Delightful," said Monsieur Puff, setting down the basket, reaching out to try and find the puppy. "He's more ghostly than I. What is his name?"

"I haven't named him yet," Clover began. "I . . ."

Achoo! Suddenly, Coco sneezed.

Achoo! Achoo! Coco sneezed again and again. Sparkly snot flew everywhere.

"Ooh la la!" cried Monsieur Puff. "This puppy—I think my dear Coco is allergic to it!"

"OHH!" cried Clover. Suddenly, it all made sense. "Coco never *did* eat any sugar-beet biscuits. She must have been allergic to the invisible puppy!"

Monsieur Puff twirled his wispy mustache. "Perhaps she has an animal allergy AND a food one. Different allergies often have similar symptoms."

"That must be it," said Clover agreeably. "I was SURE to be careful about the biscuits. Well, I'd better put the puppy inside, then."

"Oh, no need to fuss. I have to tie up Coco anyway."

Monsieur Puff led Coco far away from the puppy, slipped on her halter, and looped the lead rope around the gate.

Clover was trying to shoo the puppy away from his basket when Monsieur Puff returned.

"Coco has stopped sneezing," he announced.

"That's good," said Clover. "It's too bad she's allergic to the—"

"PUPPY!" cried a little voice.

It was Lulu. She was holding her glasses in her hand. The puppy suddenly lost interest in Monsieur Puff's basket and flew up into Lulu's arms.

"Oh, Lulu," said Leonard with his usual sigh, but then he caught sight of the floating ribbon.

"It *is* a puppy," Clover explained. "An invisible one. I think you have a few more pets than just Hickory at your house, Mr. Hue."

Leonard was speechless.

Lulu prodded him and pointed to his pocket.

"Oh . . . uh, Lulu insisted I bring you this, while it's still fresh." Leonard handed the bottle to Clover absentmindedly, still staring at the floating ribbon in his daughter's arms.

Colors swirled inside the bottle, so rich and vibrant they looked like they might burst through the glass.

They were so beautiful and mesmerizing, it was hard to look away.

"What is it?" Clover murmured.

"It's a bottled rainbow," said Monsieur Puff. "I haven't ever seen one, but I've heard of them. I wish I could create icing in such shades!"

"She's earned it," said Leonard, turning his attention back to Clover. "Marigold said you came by the house? You sure take your job seriously."

Clover blushed. "Thank you. And I'm sorry about Marigold's umbrella. I'm afraid I lost—"

BOOM. BOOM. BOOM. The ground began to tremble.

"The puppy is scared!" said Lulu, hugging the invisible creature close.

"He thinks it's thunder," Clover explained. "But it's okay. I know that sound. It's not thunder. It's—"

"Giants!" exclaimed Monsieur Puff. "Why, this party is growing bigger and bigger by the minute." Lulu giggled.

Prudence and Humphrey strode out of the Woods, wearing the largest rain hats and gumboots Clover had ever seen. Stepping over the gate, they stopped and Prudence pointed to Clover. "See," she said, taking off her rain hat and sending a shower of raindrops upon Clover and Monsieur Puff. "I told you she could take care of herself."

"I thought it was I who told *you*, my dearest diamond mine," said Humphrey gently.

"But you were the one who insisted we check on her," said Prudence, "even though I still have a headache. . . ."

"There, there, my rose garden. I thought some fresh air would do you good. But you are right. It was a terrible storm." He looked down at Clover. "Usually we aren't affected by them at all, being up so high, but this time our beanstalk was trembling."

"I just can't imagine what it must have been like down here for you," said Prudence, "being such a tiny, unmagical thing."

"Yes, are you okay, Clover?" asked Humphrey.

Clover smiled. She didn't feel bad being called tiny, or unmagical. She felt cared for.

"I'm fine, Prudence," shouted Clover. "That's really nice of you, though."

"And who might these be?" asked Prudence, gesturing to the leprechauns and the ghost. The gust of wind from her hand whisked the ghost backward.

He straightened himself up and smoothed down his mustache.

"This is Lulu and her father, Leonard. And this is Monsieur Puff."

"Monsieur Puff? The renowned baker?"

"Ooo," said Monsieur Puff, "I didn't realize giants had heard of me."

"Yes, well, we haven't tasted any of your goods, but I read an article about you in this summer's *Magical Living* magazine."

"I would be delighted to offer you a taste. Why don't you join us for a picnic?" asked Monsieur Puff. "I have plenty of cupcakes."

Prudence wrinkled her giant brow. "I don't know. We have to get back to our beanstalk. We have nothing to guard our treasure, as you know, Clover. I suppose no suitable pet has come in?"

"Oh, are you looking for a griffin?" asked Leonard. "They often guard treasure at the end of rainbows."

"Dear me, no," replied Prudence. "They are much too clawy and beaky for me. We are looking for a sweet, soft guard animal, gentle like us. But protective, of course."

Lulu shuffled over to Clover and whispered something in her ear. Clover nodded with a big smile.

"Actually, I think we do have JUST the pet for you. He's not ready for adoption yet, and still needs to be trained, but Lulu has offered to help with that."

"Really?" Prudence and Humphrey looked dumbfounded. "Where is he? *What* is he?"

Clover pointed to the floating ribbon in Lulu's arms. "This is a winged puppy. He would be the perfect guard animal, when he is bigger, and with the right training. He is invisible, so thieves wouldn't see him."

"A puppy?! Oh, how precious!" cried Prudence. "How perfect!"

"Yes, he would be. You can't adopt him yet; he is still just a puppy, and needs to grow bigger. But that shouldn't take long. And he'll get braver too, with age."

Lulu nodded, and Clover continued, "But you can visit and get to know him as he grows, and he can get to know you too."

"Well, that does sound perfect. Doesn't it, my sweet shop?" said Humphrey.

"I've always adored puppies," cooed Prudence, stooping down to pat the puppy with one finger. "Oh my!" She laughed. "I think he just licked me!"

"He must like you," said Clover. "This was all Lulu's idea, you know." She smiled at Lulu and Lulu smiled back.

"Now this calls for a celebration, doesn't it, my dumpling dish?" said Humphrey. Prudence nodded, and Monsieur Puff smiled and opened his basket.

There are few things quite as pleasant as a picnic in the sun after a hard rain. Monsieur Puff took out what Clover thought was a lacy tablecloth from his basket. But when he unfolded it—with a *poof*—it became a lovely white picnic table. Prudence sat on the grass on her rain jacket (well, actually both hers and Humphrey's jacket). As the baker set out plates, Clover fetched some tea and napkins and treats for Dipity and the puppy. She also took a treat (an apple—not a sugar-beet biscuit!) over to Coco. The little unicorn seemed fine, now that she was far enough away from the puppy. Then Clover brought out the magic kittens so they could get some sun, and set them up in a cage beside Dipity, who could keep them calm. Prudence cooed, "Oh, how very sweet," while poking a finger at the cage.

"They're very high maintenance," Clover warned, just as a spark flew off Lightning's tail and onto Prudence's giant finger.

"Ouch! Dear me! What dangers!"

"Not everything is as it seems," said Clover.

"You are certainly wise beyond your size," said Prudence.

"Mr. Jams will no doubt be very proud," added Monsieur Puff. Then he offered cupcakes to everyone, one by one, so they didn't float away. Clover, Lulu, and Leonard took chocolate ones, Humphrey strawberry, and Prudence raspberry with white icing. To the giants, the cupcakes were the size of raisins.

"Oooo," Prudence said. "That IS delicious. Humphrey, we must have him cater my next Reading Club meeting. My friends would love these cupcakes."

"But, my dear pumpkin patch," began Humphrey, "I thought the Reading Club had finished. Remember what happened last time—"

But Monsieur Puff was so pleased, he broke in, "I would be honored to cater such a magnificent event. . . ."

As Prudence and Monsieur Puff began to plan excitedly, Clover enjoyed the sun on her face and her second cupcake. It tasted even better than her first.

Too bad the last bite floated off and got stuck in the branches of a tree!

This certainly was the most peculiar picnic Clover had ever been to. Two giants sat beside two leprechauns on a weedy front lawn, with a ghost hovering in front of them. The strangest guest of all was Gump, who they had brought over to the picnic table, and who currently had a very funny look on his face. Lulu leaned over, "It's the puppy. He's licking the gnome's mustache." Clover giggled.

No matter how strange, the picnic felt perfect. And suddenly she knew the perfect name for the puppy, too.

When Picnic fell asleep on Lulu's lap, Clover carried him in. He was so soft and tiny. She quickly set up his bed in the small animals' room. She chose a cage that had room enough for Picnic to stretch his wings and that was far away from the magic kittens. Then she lined it with some blankets and the fresh feathers Cedric had delivered. She had just laid the little puppy in it when she heard a familiar voice echoing in from outside. "Great gobs of magic! What a surprise to find you all here."

It was Mr. Jams. He was back—and he sounded jolly. Clover hurried out of the room to meet him, but instead, she nearly collided with someone she had never seen before!

He was around her age and height, with brown hair that reminded Clover of a bird's nest, and serious-looking brown eyes. His complexion was pale, made paler by his

dark blue wizard robes, which fell to his feet. There were golden eggs embroidered all over them. The robes were slightly damp—and so was his hair, as though he had been caught in the storm. He was lugging an enormous suitcase that seemed as though it were filled with stones.

He pushed his glasses up his nose. "I'm looking for Clover, the one who keeps the Agency running smoothly. Mr. Jams says I should ask her to show me the egg."

Clover smiled. "*I'm* Clover. Who are you?"

The boy looked her up and down, surprised. "My name is Oliver Von Hoof. I am a magical animal expert."

Clover's mouth dropped open. THIS was the magical animal expert? She had expected an ancient man with glasses and a beard that fell to his knees. Or at least someone as old as Mr. Jams. After all, the expert had written three volumes in the *Magical Animal Encyclopedia*. But Oliver Von Hoof was no older than she was.

"You're just a boy!" she said aloud.

"And you're just a girl," said Oliver.

Clover was about to retort that she was a volunteer, which was much different than an expert, and ask how a boy could be an expert in anything, but stopped herself. If there was one thing she knew now, it was that you needed to look with your heart rather than your eyes.

And her heart said that the least she could do was give him a chance.

She stuck out her hand. Oliver eyed her warily, then shook it.

"Come on," said Clover. "Let's go get Mr. Jams. I have so much to tell him, and you too! So much has happened!"

"How long has the egg been incubating? Is it stirring? Did its spots change color? Is it making noises?"

"Not anymore." Clover paused. "It hatched."

Oliver's eyes went wide. "But . . . but . . . that's impossible," he sputtered. "I must see it at once!"

"Well," she replied, "*see* is not quite the right word."

"What do you mean?"

"Don't worry. I'll explain everything," Clover said. Then, with a smile, she added, "Welcome to the Agency."